HEY 13!

STORIES BY **GARY SOTO**

Holiday House / New York

Text copyright © 2011 by Gary Soto
All Rights Reserved
Holiday House is registered in the U.S. Patent and Trademark Office.
Printed and Bound in August 2011 at Maple Vail, York, PA, USA.
The text typeface is ITC Slimbach.
www.holidayhouse.com
First Edition
1 2 5 7 9 10 8 6 4 2

"Dirty Talk" is used by permission of Bookstop Literary Agency.

Library of Congress Cataloging-in-Publication Data

Soto, Gary.
Hey 13! / stories by Gary Soto. — 1st ed.
v. cm.
Summary: A collection of thirteen short stories about the ups and downs of
being thirteen years old.
Contents: The campus tour — Twin stars — A simple plan — Musical lives — A
very short romance — Finding religion — Celebrities — It's not nice to stare —
Whose bedroom is this? — Two girls, best friends & a frog — Altar boys —
Romancing the diary — Dirty talk.
ISBN 978-0-8234-2395-8 (hardcover)
1. Teenagers — Juvenile fiction. 2. Children's stories, American.
[1. Teenagers — Fiction. 2. Short stories.] I. Title. II. Title: Hey
thirteen!
PZ7.S7242Hf 2011
[Fic] — dc22
2011007709

To

Judy Davidson

Holmes Middle School

&

Carla Newberry

Ocoee High School

Two of the Best

CONTENTS

HEY 13!

The Campus Tour

"Stay together," Mrs. Mendel warned. "No goofing around, or you'll have to sit in the bus." She was walking backward up a service road, distributing a handout and counting the sixteen honor students from suburban Turlock. The two parent volunteers were walking ahead, talking to each other. It was a Monday morning in March, one day after a hard rain had sent the more fragile buds of the flowering trees tumbling to the ground.

Emma Fuentes shrugged her backpack onto her shoulder and half-listened to Mrs. Mendel as she bawled out two boys.

"But we haven't done anything," one student ventured.

"You were pushing each other! You think I don't have eyes?"

"But not hard," one of the culprits answered.

Mrs. Mendel muttered to the boys that they were on her list. She reversed her march and made her move to join the parent volunteers, who, out of breath, were complaining that the road was too steep.

Boys! They're such a bother, Emma brooded. She had two younger brothers, and neither could go through the living room without knocking something over. But she was determined not to dwell on them. She decided to stay happy, because the campus, she could tell as soon as she got off the bus, was so different from their junior high.

The ground was speckled with flower petals. There was a scent in the air, and the sky was the bluest she had ever seen. The main campus in the distance seemed idyllic, with trees bent over like wise old men. And was that the sound of a stream? A fountain with coins on the bottom? Whatever the source, it had a soothing effect on Emma, who during her first five years of life lived in a trailer park and the next seven in a subdivision where all the homes looked the same. Even the automated sprinklers came on at the same time, the water spilling into the gutter and racing away.

Then Emma saw a poster on a light pole that read U.S. OUT OF IRAQ, and bristled. She didn't like it one bit. No, she came from a family where the sticker on the back window of their SUV proclaimed SUPPORT OUR TROOPS. She believed in sticking up for her country's troops. Wasn't it right? Then she nearly leaped out of her shoes at a poster high above her head. The president was drawn to look like Alfred E. Neuman, the irreverent *MAD* magazine mascot. Didn't the president deserve respect? If she had been alone, taller, and possessed sharp fingernails, she would have scraped if off, angrily. It just wasn't right! The president worked hard for the country!

But Emma promised herself to keep an open mind. She was, after all, on a college campus, and wasn't that where you went to fill up your brain? And she intended to fill it, provided it was with stuff that would get her a good job.

The honor students met a college student who would be their guide. The girl yawned when she was introduced.

"Excuse me," the guide said as her eyes misted over. She poked at the corners of her eyes.

"Up late studying?" one of the parent volunteers asked.

"Nah, partying," the guide said with a chuckle. "My name is Robin."

Mrs. Mendel's mouth rippled with a smile.

But Emma refrained from smiling. Wasn't college about studying? And what was this with the guide wearing one brown sock and one red sock? And polka-dot pants? Had she rolled out of bed and just put on whatever smelly thing was the floor? Then she thought: she's probably a member of a sorority forced to wear mismatched socks. She had read about such pranks.

"I'm still sleepy," the guide admitted, and stretched. "I haven't had my coffee." She gestured for them to gather closer.

The honor students shuffled together like penguins.

"We're a liberal arts institution," Robin stated. "We were started..."

Liberal arts, Emma wondered. What does that mean? Her own father and mother didn't like liberals because liberals, they said, had too may strange ideas. But what did the guide mean by "arts"? Was this the sort of campus where they just painted all day? She would have to ask Mrs. Mendel later.

Robin led them around the campus. While the student guide pointed out buildings on campus—the campanile, the library built in 1930, the administration building that was once the college itself, the fountain designed by a famous architect—Emma saw that the guide had a chrome ball in her tongue. She grimaced and looked away when the guide's mouth opened too widely whenever she bleated a funny laugh. She thought, It must have hurt getting such a metallic doodad screwed into your tongue. She then began to wonder how she kept it clean. Did she unhook the ball from her tongue, wash it in a special solution, and then attach it once again?

"Oh, wow," Emma said under her breath. She noticed that Robin had a tattoo ringing her entire neck. It's too much, Emma silently pronounced judgment. Too hideous! She wasn't against tattoos. When she turned eighteen, she had plans to get a butterfly tattoo on her shoulder. It would be small and pretty, and a symbol of her independence.

But Emma's shock at the tattoo became a thing of the past when the guide lifted her arm to point to what was once a water tower but was now a café. Emma was horrified at the display of a bushy armpit. Didn't this person know what a razor was for? Didn't her mother teach her? Her mind began to swing wildly as she thought that maybe that's how liberals were. They didn't seem to care how they dressed or what they did to their bodies. But she reminded herself: I'm at a college. I have to be more open-minded.

"Within the college, we have a number of schools," Robin the guide was reading from a clipboard. "We have the school of education, the school of..."

But Emma's attention was drawn away by what she saw over by a fountain with water spurting from a cherub's mouth—two female college students were holding hands. She blinked. She wanted to believe that one of the girls was really a boy, but she could see that neither was. She also wanted to believe the girls were just friends, but when one kissed the other—on the cheek, but still!— Emma muttered, "Oh, my God." Her own hand went up to her cheek, as if *she* had received the kiss.

Mrs. Mendel turned and gave Emma a suspicious look.

"Nothing, Mrs. Mendel," Emma volunteered. She fluttered a pair of twinkling eyes and hoisted a smile. But she was very curious about the two girls by the fountain. She looked around at her classmates, and none of them seemed to have seen what she had seen. Were they blind? Or more worldly than she?

Emma determined not to dwell on the two girls. She told herself, This is college. I have to have an open mind. She tried to picture her forehead swinging open like a barn door. But her cheeks burned with embarrassment for those poor girls, and she wondered: Did their parents know?

"This is the commons," the guide stated. "This is where we have demonstrations."

Emma, hand over her brow to protect her eyes from the sun's rays, nearly asked, "What do you mean?"

But Mrs. Mendel asked it for the class.

"Well, it's like this." Robin explained that only last week there was a demonstration in support of Aung San Suu Kyi. The students looked at each other. One asked, "Are you speaking a different language from us?"

Robin laughed, the chrome ball on her tongue winking in the sunlight. She said no, she wasn't speaking another language. "Aung San Suu Kyi is from Myanmar. She won the Nobel Peace Prize. Do you know what house arrest is?"

"Is that like a foreclosure?" a student volunteered.

After a snorting chuckle, Robin said, "No, it's like when someone has to stay in her room for the rest of her life. That's what the government is doing to Aung San Suu Kyi. She's a big-time hero."

But that's not like prison, Emma thought. Her own room was nicely decorated, and on the shelves she had all of the stuffed animals that her father and family members had given her. She also had her own computer, her iPod, clothes in closets and drawers, and her shoes lined up against the wall like little cars. But she suddenly became uneasy. This person from Myanmar—where was Myanmar?—maybe didn't get to have these things, she figured. Maybe the house was empty, and she could only look out the front window. Maybe this house arrest thing was bad.

They walked up a small incline, the guide pointing out where the president lived. It was a small house, with a garden filled with ferns and a fountain. A caterer was knocking on the front door.

"The president?" one of the students asked.

"The president of the college," Mrs. Mendel said. "Not the president of the United States." Her face showed that she was upset with the student.

They proceeded up a grassy path. The trees and ferns still dripped with rain. The flower beds were combed but didn't hold flowers—Robin told them that in spring the garden would be bright as a pinwheel. There was a pond where the students gathered to look at koi fish moving like shadows under the water.

They're beautiful, Emma thought dreamily. She had asked her father to put a pond in their backyard, but he argued that the murky water would attract mosquitoes. Plus, it would be work. They would have to sweep out leaves and muck, and once a year drain the pond and have it scrubbed. But Emma thought that the koi were enchanting as they moved effortlessly under the greenish surface. They appeared wise, too, as many of them had long beards. Once she had her own house—she would have to go to college to afford her own house—she would put in a pond.

The honor students moved on—clumsily, as the boys kept stepping on each other's shoes.

"Up here we have the biology department," the guide began. She started to explain how the department, while small, was well-respected internationally, as it was doing important research...

But Emma tuned out the guide as she became slack-jawed watching a homeless man approaching them. His eyes were red as fresh blood in a teaspoon. His beard was the color of ashes, and in fact might have been filled with ashes from the cigarette in his gray mouth. Plus, his pants were stained beyond belief. He looked as if he had rolled around in very bright garbage and then stood up.

"Hi, Professor," the guide greeted him.

They gave each other a high-five as they passed.

Professor? Emma was bewildered. It can't be! She imagined that professors wore suits, or if not suits then at least presented themselves in nice clothes. Certainly they didn't have a ring of dirt on their collars, and this man— this professor!—had an oil slick on his collar. He could use a bar of soap and a spurt of cologne.

"What does he...teach?" Emma asked.

"Art," the guide chimed with pride. "That's my major. He's our best teacher. You should see where he lives."

Emma imagined a home on a hill, with a garden and pool with koi, and a plasma television mounted on the wall. She imagined a Lexus in the driveway and a Jaguar parked in the garage. And if he was an art professor, he would have sculptures and pretty art on the walls. But the guide told them that he lived in a school bus.

"Why?" a parent volunteer asked with a sour face. "That's worse than a trailer."

"Because he believes that we spend too much on things. He's sort of like a hippie from the 1960s. That's how I would describe him." She asked how many had noticed how skinny he was. There was a reason for that: He was a vegan, and more vegan than most because he ate only seeds.

"Like sunflower seeds?" Jason Larkin asked. "It seems like you would die living on birdseed. It's only one nutrient, and the body requires a complex food supply. And lots of liquid. We're 72 percent water, after all."

Jason, Emma admitted, was probably the smartest of the already smart group. He was good at math, and she could remember in second grade when he could spell *grandiose* and *oasis* when everyone else was still struggling to spell *friend* and *donkey*. In spite of his brain, he seldom used common sense. He talked to talk and didn't know when to be quiet, even when school bullies would press him against the wall. In such predicaments he would say things like, "You know violence has never solved anything...." She wished he would learn to button his lip.

"Yeah, like sunflower seeds," the guide answered. "He knows everything about Asian art." She scooted them along.

Soon they were across campus and standing before a modern building that was mostly glass and iron. There were twisted metal sculptures in the front that seemed like a bad car wreck from which no one walked away.

"This is the art department," the guide announced. "It looks like a hospital, and that's the point. Art's intention is to heal."

"I have to use the facility," Jason complained. "It's a matter of minutes."

Facility! Emma almost laughed. *A matter of minutes?*

Mrs. Mendel fired a stare at Jason that said, Wait!

"Like I said, this is my major," the guide said. "I do pottery. I work with clay."

Pottery, Emma wondered, as in making bowls and ashtrays?

The honor students, in pairs and threes, entered the building, which had a tropical atmosphere from all the glass. They plodded down a hallway, Emma more on tiptoes because she realized that classes were in session. She was a little upset at some of the boys who, having not been reprimanded for at least fifteen minutes, had started to push each other—Mrs. Mendel was up front and couldn't see them at their immature worst. She wished they would grow up. Weren't they the cream of the crop, as Mrs. Mendel often repeated? Sometimes, when she was on the verge of tears, she would say that they were the *scream* of the crop. Then she would scream.

But these outbursts from Mrs. Mendel weren't real. Emma understood that as a teacher she had to be on top of them. Otherwise they would make fools of themselves and their school. Mrs. Mendel was really a cool person, but sometimes she had to stoke up a fire inside her.

The honor students stopped when the guide stopped. They stood in a dark hallway.

"Let's give her all our attention," Mrs. Mendel asked. "That means you, Jason, and especially you, Michael." She scorched them with a stare.

"Thanks," Robin the guide said with a smile. She turned to the class. "The art department is world renowned..."

But Emma wasn't listening. No, she was tottering on her heels because through one of the open doors she caught sight of a naked person sitting on a tall stool. Mrs. Mendel hurried over to close the door.

I didn't see anything, Emma almost said.

"Don't worry about it," Mrs. Mendel said in a near whisper. "It's a life art class. Pay attention to our guide."

Emma turned toward the guide and even moved to the front. But her mind was on what she had briefly seen. She heard that the students drew live nude models. That's just the way it was in college. But she had to wonder where they got these nudes. They couldn't possibly be college students. She would just die if she had to sit naked in a chair and let other people draw her. She winced at the thought of her body, all 103 pounds, on the Internet, on someone's Facebook page! She closed her eyes momentarily and envisioned herself naked with people staring at her! No way! She would die first!

"Come on," Mrs. Mendel called. "Don't linger, Emma."

Emma pulled out of her shock and caught up with the students making their way down the hall, though she did turn and look at the closed door where the model was being drawn.

Soon they were in the music building, where somewhere an oboe was making a bird-like call to a flute in another room. A piano was being played. No, two pianos were being played. And a kettledrum was being pounded like a bad headache.

"Who plays an instrument?" the guide asked.

More than half of the honor students raised their hands.

Emma was surprised at Jason Larkin's raised hand. She knew he was super smart (ask him about a computer program and his fingers would fly over the keyboard), but she had never seen him carry a musical instrument.

"What do you play?" the guide asked Jason.

"I don't play an instrument. I have to use the facility. My minutes are up. It's not humanly possible to contain this bladder of mine." To make this point he began to hop and squirm.

Everyone laughed, including Mrs. Mendel, who said, "Okay, I give up. Nature calls. If you must, go!" She waved him off and wagged her head and muttered, "These kids..."

Jason trotted off down the hall, and two other boys followed.

"The scream of the crop," Mrs. Mendel told the two parent volunteers, who had to laugh. To the honor students she said, "And the rest of you, go if you have to go.

We'll take a little break." She told the guide that she was doing a really fine job, but the students needed a break.

"Cool," Robin remarked. "I'll run over to get myself a coffee."

"You have ten minutes," Mrs. Mendel told the students. "It's okay, but don't wander too far. Try to stay together."

Emma hooked arms with Alicia, her best friend in this pack. They walked from the art building and out onto the commons, where a tai chi class was being conducted under a magnolia tree. The two girls approached the group and stood half in, half out of the shadows of the large flowering tree. Emma looked in silence at the beautifully strange movements. She could see herself doing tai chi, and found her arm lifting in front of her as she imitated a movement.

"What are you doing?" Alicia asked.

"I don't know," she answered. Her arm dropped like an ax.

"Join us," the instructor said. She had fallen out of line and was waving for them to step among them. "Just follow along."

Emma looked at Alicia and begged in a whisper, "Come on. Let's try."

"No, you go." Alicia backed away.

"Come on. Just for a little bit?"

Alicia stepped back, her fingers coming to her mouth. She shook her head no.

Emma decided to give it a try. She took off her socks and shoes, tiptoed onto the still wet lawn, and mingled among the students, most of whom were female. She followed the person to the left, then right, as they moved slowly in something like a dance.

"Breathe naturally," the leader said. "Breathe from your center."

Breathe naturally? Emma wondered. Wasn't breathing always natural? And where was her center? Then she realized that she had been holding her breath. She relaxed, let air enter her parted lips, and momentarily closed her eyes. Her center, she could feel, was around her belly button. Why hadn't she known that?

"Think of yourself as water," the leader told the students. "Let your arms flow. Turn and pivot to your left."

"Like water," Emma murmured as she turned with a stumble toward the left. She saw her arms as water and her body as water, and imagined for a brief moment a small river. She saw blue behind her lids and saw herself doing it—*tai chi*—on her front lawn at home. She could feel the grass under her feet and hear the fountain.

"Breathe," the leader said.

Breathe, Emma told herself.

"Think down, think center," the leader added.

Think down, think center, Emma instructed her body.

"Find your balance," the leader instructed. "Let the *chi* flow through your limbs."

Balance, she thought. Her mind was quieting, as just

before sleep, when Mrs. Mendel yelled, "Everyone! Come on!" Her voice was anything but flowing water and the thing called center—more like two pot lids crashing to the kitchen floor.

Emma left the tai chi group, pulling her socks and shoes back on, and waved good-bye to the leader, who nodded as a sign of good-bye. She stopped to tie her shoes and wonder what *tai chi* meant, the words themselves.

"Emma, don't linger," Mrs. Mendel said none too nicely. "Let's catch up."

Emma hurried up and joined the group. They were headed off to the gymnasium, she learned, which was large as a cathedral. Robin told the group that they didn't have organized sports, just volleyball and soccer, but they won a championship—Robin looked down at the clipboard— they won a volleyball championship in 1998.

That's when I was born, Emma said to herself. She thought it was a good year to be born. Anytime earlier, and the world wouldn't have had all the things to play with. She thought of her cell phone, which was turned off for the morning but which she knew held breathy messages from friends.

But they didn't make it the gymnasium. Robin, the guide, led them to the front of the administration building, where a knot of students were handing out leaflets. Tiptoeing, Robin hugged and kissed a boy whom Emma assumed was her boyfriend, or at least someone she liked well enough. Even without the kiss she would have guessed they were an item, as their eyes were locked on each other.

"Will I see you later?" the boyfriend asked.

"After this?" she said, and touched his sleeve. "No, I gotta to do another one."

After this? No, I gotta do another one? Emma was put off that Robin didn't dip her voice into a whisper. Were she and her classmates such a bother? Earlier she was ready to forgive their guide's sloppy dress, but not now!

But her moodiness disappeared when a bearded young man stepped among the honor students and began handing out leaflets. He fist-bumped a few of the students, and gave peace signs to others. He was thin as a rake, and had green eyes that were large and clear, as if unused.

"Where are you from?" he asked.

"From Turlock," the honor students sang.

"Oh," Emma muttered, a pink blush blooming on her cheeks. Secretly she saw herself easily liking him. He was older but cute, and his voice was deep and confident. He could explain himself clearly. He told them about global warming, which was nothing new to Emma. She had written a paper about global warming, and had read on the Internet that, at the current rate of the icebergs melting, in eighty years the ocean would rise and spill into the valley where she lived. And the poor polar bears? The penguins, all the arctic birds? Where would they go?

"The government needs to listen to nature," the young man stated.

Listen to nature? she wondered. How? We could hear animals in nature—the howl of coyotes came to mind—and we could hear the ocean roar and wind slice through redwoods. But how do you listen to nature?

"Corporations are responsible," he continued. "We're all responsible. We're consuming too much."

Emma swallowed this bit of truth. There was no arguing that if she went into her garage she would find two of everything, a sort of Noah's ark of consumer stuff.

"We're with California for a Strong Environment. We need you to call your congressperson, your senator, even your mayor."

Emma was tongue-tied at the suggestion of calling someone like a congressperson. She scowled at the leaflet and, yes, there were the telephone numbers of elected officials. How did he get these numbers? She swallowed. She could barely talk to the school principal—it was something that made her nervous—and now this bearded person wanted her to pester these important people? The leaflet seemed to wilt like lettuce in her hand.

But the honor students didn't seem interested in what he had to say. One by one they were drawn away to a dog catching a Frisbee.

"They don't care, do they?" Emma said. She was envisioning in the back of her mind a senator sitting behind a large desk. He was bald, in a suit, and red in the face from doing...doing just what? He couldn't be sweating from signing papers.

"No, most of them don't," the young man answered. "They just talk. They eat lunch. They pal around. But our generation needs to make a stand now. I know it sounds like an old cliché, but we can make a change. It's a matter of lifestyle." He mentioned bicycle power and electric cars, and eco-friendly houses that use little water, and solar panels that can run appliances.

"Is your beard real?" Alicia asked.

Emma could have fallen over. Her cheeks reddened in embarrassment for Alicia. *Is your beard real?* What kind of question is that? she almost snapped at Alicia.

The young man smiled. "Yes, it's real." She stroked it and gave it a tug.

Alicia laughed, said it looked fake, and ran to join the others, and Emma wondered, What is wrong with her? That was so rude! And childish! There was nowhere to hide, except by lowering her head and reading the leaflet.

"Do you want to sign this petition?"

Petition? Emma wondered as she looked up. He was cute, and real. He believed in what he was saying. It was truer than what most grown-ups had to say.

The young man held out a clipboard. She took it and signed the petition, giving her full name of Emma Sara Fuentes.

"I want to do something," she told the young man. "I know I'm only in middle school, but I will. You'll see."

"That's cool," he said with a smile.

Waving the leaflet at him, she promised to call the

elected officials. She turned, skipped in happiness, and joined her classmates.

They finished the tour of the campus, ate lunch on the grass, and talked about what they had learned.

"You were well-behaved," Mrs. Mendel said. "I'm proud of you."

Well-behaved? Emma was beginning to wonder whether college was about being well-behaved. She finished her apple, rose from the lawn, and from her back pocket took out the leaflet. She looked at the names of the congresspersons and senators, and then brought out her cell phone from her backpack. Then she remembered that using cell phones on the campus tour was forbidden. That was fine by her. She would make the call when she was alone, and speak her mind about polar bears and ice caps. Right now she was watching Jason, on all fours, barking like a dog. One of the boys was tossing the Frisbee to see if Jason could catch it in his mouth.

She had to laugh. Jason was funny and maybe would one day become like the guy with the beard. But right now he was on his knees doing a good job of pretending to be a dog.

At one o'clock the bus pulled out of the parking lot. It groaned up a hill, the gears shifting from first to second. Soon they would be on the freeway, heading home. Emma counted her blessings: mom and dad still together, her little brothers who fell over like bowling pins when they fought, a bedroom of her own, and a future. Yes, she was one among sixteen, and one of the smartest. She had seen political posters, girls holding hands, a professor who lived on sunflower seeds, a nude person, tai chi, students who were really odd, and the young man in a beard, wiser than his years.

The bus moved like a large yellow whale as it sped along freeway 580. The city gave way to suburbs, then orchards and fields, and then another patch of suburbs. Emma was going home, but she had seen the kind of college where she would like to go. She sat with her own thoughts. She remembered that she wanted to ask, What's *tai*? What's *chi*? She would have time, she figured. She was only thirteen, and already had learned that her center was around her navel and that there were young men, some bearded and others cleanly shaved, speaking in kind tones about helping the world.

Twin Stars

Teri and Luz were better known as the Glitz Girls de Southeast Fresno, and known to be with each other 24/7. They were like twins, inseparable, and even strolled with their arms interlocked. They liked the same music, the same clothes, and the same hairstyles. One late afternoon they closed the bedroom door, crowded before a mirror hanging over a cluttered chest of drawers, and put on makeup, lots of it, so much that their eyes, lips, and cheeks appeared injured.

"How do I look?" Luz asked. She was blinking at the mirror.

"Like you fell off Rudy's board, girl," Teri answered.

Rudy was a boy Luz liked for a week, and after that week, which she thought lasted longer than beans boiling on the stove, she told him adios and shoved him off on his board. She told him, after she saw him funky from playing basketball with his friends, that she liked him but not the way he liked her. She demanded a boyfriend who smelled good. Was that asking too much?

"Like shut up!" Luz returned playfully. Then she stiffened, her eyes spooked. "Oh, my gosh! That's what we'll call our first hit!" She jumped up and down with her right hand held high as if she were holding a microphone.

Teri had attached one of her mother's false eyelashes, and was now struggling with the second one. It was like trying to attach a spider to your eyelid. How did anyone wear them? she wondered. She gave up, made a face at the false eyelash, and turned to Luz. "What do you mean?"

"The title of our first hit. Like 'Shut Up.' "

"*Loca*, shut up yourself."

"No, not 'Shut Up' like you." Luz squeezed her friend to her body. She pulled away, excited. "Our song will be called 'Shut Up.' Don't you see?"

Teri struggled with momentary confusion. Had this wobbly feeling to do with how one eye was unadorned and the other heavy with false lashes?

"We're going to write a song," Luz said as she began to hunt through her desk for something to write with.

"We are?"

"Yes!" She located a school pencil. "This here is going to be worth a lot of money." She held up the pencil.

"That? The pencil? Get out of here." Teri laughed, exposing a wad of gum on her molars. "That's too funny."

"No, I'm serious. We can write songs and then later

when we're famous sell the pencil on eBay." She then bit the pencil like a beaver. "Now you do it."

Teri stepped back as she brought her hands to cover her mouth. She was afraid that Luz might jam the pencil down her throat. The girl was just crazy.

"Bite the pencil. Leave your mark on it." She explained that their teeth marks would be embedded in the pencil and then it would be worth thousands.

"Who would buy that ugly thing?" Teri asked.

"Somebody rich! You wait!"

Teri laughed again, this time choking on her gum. She spit it out into her palm, looked at the gleaming pile, and then wadded it up in a Kleenex.

"Yeah," Luz breathed dreamily as she pocketed the pencil. "We write a song, get someone to record us, and then we'll be in magazines."

"And on TV!"

"That's it! Let's think *American Idol*. People will go crazy when they see us." She wiggled her hips.

"And on the Internet!"

The two girls hugged and jumped in a circle. They were out of breath when Teri spoiled the moment by saying that she didn't know how to write lyrics.

"We'll learn," Luz argued weakly. But her brow became rumpled with worry. Her fingernails leaped to her mouth, and she chewed.

"You're going to ruin your nails." She playfully slapped Luz's hand. "Stop it!"

"Oh, oh, oh!" Luz screamed as she took Teri's hand. "That's the name of our second international hit."

"What?"

" 'Stop it!' That's our second hit."

The two girls jumped around, dislodging Teri's false eyelash into an unnatural position. After they calmed down Luz took the pencil from her pocket and located her Hello Kitty tablet. They sat on the edge of Teri's bed.

"You write the first line," Teri said. She was nervous writing with someone—even her best friend—looking on.

"Why me?" Luz asked.

" 'Cause you talk more than me."

Then Luz, leaping from the bed, issued another "Oh, oh, oh."

"What?" Teri asked.

"Our third song can be 'Why me?' "

"Give me that," Teri demanded, and took the pencil. She bit it like corn on the cob, moving the pencil around and around until it was dented with deep teeth marks on all sides. She wiped the pencil on her pants and handed it back to Luz.

"Teri, you must be hungry," she remarked as she examined the pencil. She then crowed, "Oh, oh, oh. Our fourth hit! We'll call it . . . 'Hungry for You.' " She snapped her fingers. "That's it. 'Hungry for You, Hungry for you, Baby.' " Her body began to sway as she hummed.

Teri joined in by snapping her fingers and swaying her body. But where were the lyrics? she wondered. She listened to music on her iPod more than she listened to people, but could she compose lyrics?

Luz went through her purse and brought out a red whip. She measured its length, and pulled it until it snapped into two. "This is like our contract," Luz said.

Teri took her half and immediately set her teeth to yanking off a piece. The red whip stretched and snapped.

"You get half of what we make, and I get the other half." Luz laughed and stuffed some of the licorice into her mouth.

Teri chewed her red whip until it was all gone. She lifted her eyes toward the ceiling, where there was an old poster of a rock group that broke up and went, one by one, into rehab. They had been like gods when she and Luz were seven years old, and earned a space on their ceiling, where all gods belonged as they looked down at their worshipers.

"I like it," Teri concluded. She liked the idea of someone hungering for another person so much that her stomach began to rumble. She pressed a palm against her tummy to quiet the commotion.

Luz smiled. She was glowing.

Teri stared at her friend. She always sensed that Luz was smart, but now she was thinking that maybe Luz had a special verbal power. The girl could come up with song titles just like that.

But what about the rest of the song? Teri wondered as she carefully peeled off the wayward false eyelash. She asked, "But we got to do the words first. . . . Who's going to play the music?"

"Don't worry," Luz remarked. She brought out her cell phone. "Take a picture of me."

In the dusty shadows of the bedroom, Teri snapped two photos of Luz writing on the notepad. She took a picture of Luz standing by the window. Luz next lay on her back, one leg crossed over the other, and stared upward at the rock poster. She told Teri that they had to have a look where they appeared hurt by some boy and were really sad and would be sad until the end of eternity. Then she leaped from the bed and began to jump up and down, repeating, "Oh, oh, oh."

By now Teri knew the routine.

"Not another song," Teri remarked.

"No, no. I'm thinking that maybe we need to get two other girls in our group." She explained that most girl groups had at least three members, but the Spice Girls had four—and look at them, Luz argued. They were rich, had gorgeous boyfriends or husbands, and couldn't go anywhere without people saying, "Hey, you look familiar. Are you famous?" She laughed and said, "We'll be walking around Fresno and people will be saying, 'Hey, it's the Glitz Girls.' "

"Walking?" Teri asked.

"You're right. Once we're rich, we'll be in a limo!" She had her hands raised as if holding a steering wheel.

"Driving?" Teri asked. "No, girl, someone drives *us!*"

Giddy, they hugged each other.

"Who do you think should join us?" Teri was already thinking of Yolanda Sanchez, a girl from school who could sing, dance, and play piano. Plus she was pretty and her teeth were white as Chiclets. But Teri knew that Yolanda was a show-off and would probably want to be the leader. Teri could see it. They could start off at the Fresno District Fair, maybe right next to where they keep cows and sheep, and within a year they would be on television! She knew Yolanda would hog the camera—with those big white teeth of hers!—and the only thing they would show of Luz and Teri would be their arms!

So Teri wasn't surprised when Luz said, "How about Yolanda?"

"Nah, not her," Teri answered. She produced a sour expression to say emphatically that Yolanda was out before she was in.

"How about Chantel?" Luz suggested next.

Teri sucked in her lower lip, let her mind assess the suggestion, and after six seconds of deliberation shook her head no. She also shook her head to Lolly, Jasmine, Dakota, Erika from science class, Erika from English, and the three Lupes they knew.

"Who, then?" Luz asked.

Teri didn't bother to answer. No, if they were going to be the Glitz Girls de Southeast Fresno, it would be just the two of them. They had been friends since they were babies and crawling around the lawn with grass on their drooling tongues. Now they were thirteen, though they sometimes said they were fourteen, or even fifteen if their eyelashes stayed put.

"Let's go outside," Teri suggested.

They wiped the heavy makeup off their faces so Teri's mother wouldn't grimace at the sight of them.

"And we were looking so *hot*," Luz said as she rubbed her cheeks with a Kleenex.

After they were done they tiptoed into the kitchen and snagged a couple of sodas. They next rummaged through the pantry, snagging a half-eaten bag of chips. Silent as cats, they exited by the kitchen door and plopped down on the front lawn. It was seven in the evening, still so hot that the mosquitoes had not yet lifted into the air to pester people. The sun was a red-eyed Cyclops slowly closing its fiery lid.

"Wouldn't it be great," Teri mumbled. She pushed her hand into the bag of chips. She tossed them into her mouth. "To be on TV."

"On the radio, too," Luz added. "We've got to create our own web page." She popped open her soda and chugged. She burped.

"Like...crude," Teri teased as she pulled up blades of grass.

Luz burped a second time, this time besting her first effort. She snorted and said that the soda almost got up her nose.

"Like gross," Teri said, scooting back on her bottom.

"It's the soda."

"Luz, there could be somebody taking your picture right now! We'll be all over the web." She tossed the grass at Luz.

Luz looked around, playing with her hair. "Who's going to take our picture? Plus, Teri, in some cultures it's okay to burp."

"But you're not from that culture. You're from Fresno."

"People burp here. We got our slobs!" Luz laughed and then stopped when she saw Rudy coming up the street on his board. She composed herself, sitting straight up and hiding the bag of chips behind her.

"Hey," Rudy greeted them as he slowed, popped the board into the crook of his arm, and joined the two girls on the lawn. "What are you doing?"

Teri looked at Luz. Should we say that we're writing songs? her gaze asked.

"Chilling," Luz answered. "You're all sweaty."

"Been wrestling with Cody," Rudy explained, and wiped his face by pulling up the front of his T-shirt. "We're getting into mixed martial arts. Like I got three bruises."

"You know karate?" Teri asked.

"A little bit. I got a yellow belt," Rudy answered, then patted spit on a scratch on his forearm. "But mixed martial arts is everything, like boxing and wrestling and jumping on people all together." He had said all this while his eyes were nailed on Teri's soda. He asked, "Can I have a drink? I'm thirsty."

"Have mine," Luz volunteered, lifting hers with two hands like a chalice.

Rudy took the soda and chugged it, came up for air, and burped. He then emptied the contents and crushed the can. "My grip is getting really strong." He told the girls how he lifted weights and figured that by the time school started he could probably hang from his roof by his fingertips.

"Why would you want to do that?" Luz asked.

"Nah, I don't want to. I'm just saying that if I fell off my roof, I could like grip the roof and hang there." He then stated that maybe in two years he could probably hang onto a plane's wing when it took off.

The girls looked at each other. They hid their faces when they laughed.

"It's not funny. You don't know when you might have to hang onto an airplane wing. It happens."

"Yeah, I read about it," Teri said, trying hard not to burst with laughter.

Rudy said that it would be about four years before his parents would allow him to get into the cage—the place where they did the mixed martial arts—but he could wait because he still had to put on muscle and learn how to kick higher than waist level. His eyes then fell upon Teri's soda.

"Go ahead," Teri offered. "You want some chips?"

Rudy said yes to the chips and then to the breath mint that Luz offered. He stood up and climbed the lower branches of the tree in the front yard. He held on by his fingertips, his T-shirt worked up so that his belly was showing.

"See what I mean?" Rudy said in a strained voice. "I could probably hang like this for about two days." He let go, swatted and examined his palms, and flopped down next to the girls.

Teri wished that Rudy would leave and allow Luz and her to get back into the groove of coming up with song titles. She could see why Luz had dumped him—he was funky! Once again he wiped his face by pulling up his shirt. Finally, after ten minutes of his crowing about death holds in mixed martial arts, he left. But first he took the empty soda cans, attached them to his shoes, and walked around on the sidewalk. His clanging steps made enough noise for Teri's father to part the front drapes and look out. He frowned but didn't come outside.

"I used to do this when I was five," Rudy said, his arms out for balance.

Teri thought, Wasn't that like eight years ago? No wonder Luz dumped him. So sweaty and immature.

In time Rudy rode off on his board. The girls were left alone, but the mood had changed and their musical career was stalled. They couldn't think of any words to put down on paper.

"He messed us up," Luz lamented. She munched on the last flakes of chips, her mouth moving like a rabbit's.

"Oh, oh, oh," Teri yelled. "How about 'Messed Up'?"

Since Luz had come up with all the titles so far, she thought that maybe it was her turn to be creative. And she was creative, but usually with her hands. She was known for her clay ashtrays, beadwork, and the lanyards she made at Holmes playground.

Luz nixed that title. She didn't want to be a rapper-like songster, and "Messed Up" sounded like someone who didn't do well in school.

They lay on the grass. It had been a long day. They had gone to the mall, eaten two hamburgers each, sucked on diet sodas until their stomachs tumbled with the brown liquids, watched ten minutes of a bad movie called "Kung Fu Grandpas," and, best of all, been with each other. They had tried on each other's clothes and worn false eyelashes in private. They had become songwriters—or at least had come up with the titles and a few of the lines when Luz began to sing, "You came by / to say hi / to say you're going into the cage / the big, big rage . . . Shut up."

The girls rolled on the grass and laughed until tears squeezed from the corners of their eyes like juice from a lemon. Teri said that she could feel the earth spinning and they just might fly into the sky. She gripped the ground and said, "Hey, I'm like Rudy holding on!"

"You're bad," Luz said. "Making fun of my ex!" She tossed a handful of grass blades at Teri. She then blurted, "Hey, did you see that?" Luz pointed skyward.

Teri had seen it—a shooting star. It burned bright, but was brief as two counts of a blinking eye. "Yeah, I saw it."

Luz said, "Oh, oh, oh!" She sat up, her necklace bouncing as she got more excited. "That's the title of our biggest hit!"

Teri sat up. "Okay, what's it called?"

"Burning Star," Luz answered. She had made a fist and let the fist rise slowly and then explode—the fingers were twinkling stars falling earthward. She told Teri the song was about a relationship between a girl and a guy, and that the guy was thinking that love is like a star. Love sometimes explodes and is over. After that there's just darkness, just like space.

"But do stars explode?" Teri asked.

Confused, her brow wrinkling with doubt, Luz answered, "I don't know." Then her frown suddenly lifted. She pointed: "Did you see them?"

Teri had. She saw two shooting stars, and for a second she thought of themselves—her and Luz—as singers whose career had come and gone. But she didn't say anything. She just lay on the grass, at peace with her best friend. The valley wind was beginning to rattle the leaves on the tree. She let her mind wander, let it think that the leaves were like fans, and they were applauding the Glitz Girls de Southeast Fresno.

A Simple Plan

First the cats went. Saul Garcia's father took them somewhere—the pound, Saul hoped, a family member, he prayed, but most likely a country road, he feared. There the cats, all youngish, were probably abandoned, meowing with their furry faces lifted skyward, and finally scampering into the tomato fields when a truck passed. Then the goat they kept in a makeshift corral was sold, lifted into the back of the truck, and driven away while the animal was still eating a mouthful of hay. Then his three chickens were given to Señor Rodriguez, the man across the street. Saul could see them in a rickety coop, and then a day later the chickens were gone. Had they become Sunday soup for a family of seven?

"That's messed up," Saul said under his breath. He imagined the chickens being grabbed, tucked under an arm, and then...he couldn't will away the ugly image inside his mind. He scrubbed his eyes with his fists. He felt like crying. They had been his chickens, and now they were gone.

The Garcias were moving from their country neighborhood outside of Fresno—creaky and unpainted houses, trailers parked one against the other, and collapsed canvas army tents where farmworkers once lived. It was a dusty place, a former migrant camp the rumor had it, but to Saul it was home. His best friend, Marcos Mendez, lived in one of the trailers, and they spent their time riding bikes and kicking around the canal. Marcos owned a BB gun, and they would shoot things that were not living—road signs and bottles that shattered. They took target practice, aiming at cans and even litter—potato chip bags that had blown from town all the way to the country.

Now his father wanted Saul to get rid of Lucky, their old dog with arthritis in his bones.

"I can't, *Papi*," Saul said, then lowered his face. "*No puedo.*" He was ready to cry and beg his father that he would do anything if Lucky could come with them. He was ready to run away with the dog. It was just too cruel!

His father, a rough man, had a job in a dairy, and was definitely country. Born on a rancho in Zacatecas, Mexico, he had worked with his hands since he was nine years old. Saul could recite all his stories, sometimes delivered when his father was drunk and with eyes scary as the reddest salmon eggs. How many times had he told the story of crossing the border at Nogales, with Pepsi bottles filled with water? What had his father had in his pockets? *Nada.*

What had he eaten for three days as he hid from *la migra*? *Nada*. His father first worked as a dishwasher in a Chinese restaurant (he would never eat Chinese food again), then in a used battery shop (a battery exploded and splattered acid that scarred his hands), and finally arrived in the San Joaquin Valley, where he worked tomatoes and canta-loupes, plus fixed cars on the side, and, in the early days when they were really poor, collected plastic bottles and aluminum cans at Kearny Park. His father was a worker, with a belly spilling over his cowboy belt, but in no way a weak man. His brow was darkened by sun and his hair whipped by wind—elements of nature he lived under. When he smiled, which was rare, a gold tooth revealed itself.

"*¿No puedes hacerlo?*" his father asked sternly. "You can't do it? He's old, he's no good!" His mouth was hidden by a large, droopy mustache, and his eyes were so narrow that no light shone on their pupils. His father told them that he shouldn't be a baby, that at thirteen it was time for him to grow up! His father scolded Saul as the two stood at the truck. The hood was raised, and his father was changing a fan belt.

Saul could say only, "But he's my dog." A lump formed in his throat, and his eyes were ready to puddle.

But his father, with hands oily from the fan belt, mocked his son. He said that he had to be a man, that life was not always MacDonald's hamburgers.

When was life ever hamburgers? Saul argued silently.

His father never took them anywhere. His father worked at a dairy, rising before there was light and arriving home nine hours later with flies on his shoulders and smelling of cow dung. If they went anywhere it was to his *compa*'s house in West Fresno, where Saul and his sister, Rebecca, would sit on the couch, both of them nearly comatose from boredom.

"But Lucky..."

"Lucky nothing! You take him away!" his father scolded.

His father was stern, and possibly mean at heart, though Saul tried to think of his father as a practical man. He could fix their truck, do the plumbing when the pipes choked up, oversee a garden, and even sew—late at night, on an ancient sewing machine and with his reading glasses on his nose, he would make slipcovers for couches and chairs and sell them at swap meets.

But could his father love? Could he feel how he felt, a boy's love for his dog?

Just because they were moving, his father wanted to get rid of Lucky. He couldn't leave Lucky behind because the neighbors would later complain. No, they had to do it right. Clean up the house, do a dump run, and hand the keys back to the landlord, a spidery man who lived in one of the trailers.

"Just take him out to the country," Saul's father ordered.

So Saul approached Lucky, who was on the back porch

licking a paw. Lucky looked up, his eyes mirroring the image of Saul as he bent down. When he stroked his dog's head Lucky began to wag his tail slowly.

"I have to," Saul told Lucky. "He's making me."

Saul's sister, seven-year-old Rebecca, came out onto the porch. Although it was one in the afternoon, she was still in her princess pajamas and wearing slippers the color of bananas. She cradled a doll in her arms.

"Don't do it," Rebecca begged. She had a whimper in her voice, and her eyes were ready to drip tears. Lucky was his dog, but she loved him, too. She would sometimes roast him a hot dog on a fork, blow on it until it cooled, and then let Lucky eat from the fork. He had nice manners, better than most people.

Saul muttered, "It's not fair."

Rebecca got down on her knees, hugged Lucky, and cried that he was a brave dog, a good dog, a pretty dog. She ran out of words as she let go of Lucky. She disappeared back into the house, holding the doll by its hair.

From the porch Saul scanned the neighborhood—six houses, fourteen trailers, broken-down cars and trucks, oil drums, tires and rusty chrome rims, sofas and mattresses, scraggly gardens, other dogs either leashed to clotheslines or wandering the road, noses poking at litter in the gutter. Saul liked where he lived, though he knew it wasn't pretty and people driving down the road on the way to Fresno probably thought it was ugly. It wasn't ugly. The wind blew through the neighborhood, the sun burned, and the neighbors were like neighbors anywhere—kind, mean, quiet, or loud. Laundry in each yard whipped from clotheslines. Wasn't that a sign they were clean people?

"Let's go," Saul called to Lucky, who rose to his floppy legs, panting. He trotted next to Saul as they left the yard and ambled down the street. Saul waved to Señor Rodriguez, who was in his yard clipping a rose-bush. Señor Rodriguez waved a thorny hand back at him.

Saul couldn't look down at Lucky. He couldn't say a word when Angel Flores, a little boy with a hole in his heart, asked if he wanted to play football. Angel was holding a child-sized football. Any other time Saul would have stopped and played with him, even if it was boring just tossing the ball underhand so that Angel could catch it and run for a touchdown. Angel, people said, wasn't going to live long.

Soon Saul was leaping over a small rivulet from an irrigation ditch. He stopped at the runoff, which was thin as a wrist. There were polliwogs squirming in the clear water. There were hundreds of them, all of them knocking against each other, determined to survive. In six months some would have become bloated frogs hidden in the weeds around the ditch.

Saul had once seen a man gig for frogs with a long spear-like pole. He would thrust his pole at a frog, catch it on the end, and place it in a burlap sack. How they were cooked—in boiling water or in a pan with their legs spread out—Saul couldn't imagine.

Lucky drank from a puddle, with his feet in the puddle. He was a sweet old animal, one who never complained at hardships, though one time when he came across a dead dog in the road he raised his head skyward and howled. It was a better expression of love than most people could muster—or so Saul believed.

When Saul whistled, Lucky gazed up, water dripping from his jaw. His tail was moving.

"Let's go," Saul said, and hurled a rock in the air, over the dog, in the direction of a landlocked seagull. The seagull leaped and came down. Saul had to wonder about how—and why!—the seagull had come into the valley. The Pacific Ocean was over a ridge of coastal mountains that could be seen on clear days. A group of seagulls sat in the fields, occasionally flapping to and fro behind tractors. But mostly they dotted the landscape, white bundles against the rich earth.

Saul and Lucky followed the rivulet until it gave out. They scrambled over a gully, opened and closed a barbed-wire gate, and followed a tractor path onto a hard field. To the left there were acres of recently planted cotton plants so small they could be called babies. That's how Saul would describe them—baby plants. But he was sure that his father would laugh at him for that description.

To the right was a field cut with rows of baby corn. It was March, still rainy season. In time the corn would stretch skyward and rustle in the valley wind. By late July combines would be brought in, and all night the machines would sweep through the fields, their scissor-like teeth pulling the corn into their metal mouths.

When Lucky barked, Saul looked up and noticed a figure in the distance. When the figure waved, Saul kept his hands as his sides and thought for a second of walking the other way, in a hurry maybe. In the country you could never tell who was out there, in the brush or hiding in the arroyo—an escaped convict from Avenal once lived in the fields, surviving on corn and ditch water. But he was caught and hauled away, the color of burnt toast from the sun. They said he was in jail for killing a man.

But when Saul noticed that Lucky was wagging his tail and whimpering in a friendly way, he gathered there was no reason to fear.

Slowly the approaching figure became Marcos, his best friend from the neighborhood. Marcos was toting his BB gun.

"Hey," Marcos greeted him. He was breathing hard. "I thought it was you." He looked down at Lucky. "Is your father making you?" He was dressed in a Bakersfield State sweatshirt and jeans flecked with mud. His shoes were muddy, his face nearly dark as mud.

"Yeah," mumbled Saul. "I don't know why. I know a neighbor would take him."

Marcos didn't say anything. He squatted, frog-like, and took Lucky's snout into his hand and wagged it.

Whimpering, Lucky worked his way free as he backpedaled. He began to wag his tail, because everyone was his friend. He rolled his tongue over his mouth.

"Man, he's a cool dog," Marcos stated. But he explained that his father didn't like animals, unless they were on his plate.

Saul was too weak from sadness to smile at this little joke—animals on a plate, as in pork chops, hamburger, chicken. He stood with his hands at his sides and gazed toward the distance, where he would have to walk, none too happily. He turned: the clutch of houses and trailers where he and Marcos lived was a mile, a mile and a half, away. Smoke rose from there—a barbecue? Debris raked into a pile and lit? Farther west, clouds were rolling over the coastal range and heading east. They would reach the valley, perhaps drench them with rain, but mostly likely keep rolling toward the Sierra Nevada.

"I have to go," Marcos said. "Bye, fella." He bent down and stroked Lucky's head. He scratched the hanging fur under his chin.

Saul could see Marcos's reflection in Lucky's pupils. He began to think that animals were nicer than people. Poor cows, he almost said aloud. They have to be with my father. Saul suspected that his father shouted and pushed them around, maybe even hit them with sticks, and they had to endure his father's brutishness through their mooing. But who heard the cows' bellowing?

Saul closed his eyes and pictured a frog on the end of a makeshift spear. He saw his chickens, too, and a knife rising to cut their throats. And their cats? They were kicked out of his father's truck on a country road and now living on mice in the tomato fields.

"This is messed up," Marcos remarked. He stood in silence with wind whistling across the low-lying weeds. He told Saul that his mother was mad at him because he had washed an orange pillowcase with whites, and now the whites were rust colored. He asked Saul if he had seen their laundry. Where they lived—the six houses, the fourteen trailers—everyone's laundry could be seen if you looked.

"Nah, I didn't see it," Saul answered.

"She's mad," Marcos said. "I'm mad, too. She doesn't understand."

Understand what? Saul almost asked.

Then it became clear to Saul. They were becoming teenagers, and sometimes made mistakes. They couldn't help it. Lamps toppled over when they entered living rooms. Beans were burnt under their watch. Muddy tracks appeared on the kitchen floor. Gym clothes were lost, and the milk left out on the counter. Sometimes they missed the school bus, but what did it matter? What was the big deal of washing an orange pillowcase with white underwear?

"I really got to go," Marcos said, and petted Lucky once more.

When he started to walk away, Saul suddenly became aware that his friend had the gait of a worker. He moved with a roll in his shoulders and with short steps. Was this his destiny? To work in the fields, in a dairy? He watched his friend stumble down the ditch bank, his head barely visible and then gone. He hoped that the laundry would be dry by the time he got home, pulled from the clothesline, and that Marcos's mother would have moved on, like a cloud, to other brooding complaints.

Saul whistled at Lucky, who had located a gopher hole and was poking his nose at its entrance. Tail wagging, he barked at the hole until Saul told him to be quiet. The dog looked up, then back at the hole, and finally joined Saul, who was moving in quick steps.

They walked a mile over ground damp from last night's rain. In a few weeks the ground would harden and the wind would peel the dirt and lift it skyward. But now it just stuck to his sneakers. In a slow run he maneuvered around tumbleweeds, thinking of himself as a running back. He followed a dry rivulet that rain had etched in the ground, and stopped once to poke his sneaker at some bones bleached by the sun. To him they looked like cat bones—the skull was slender. The years had pulled the fur from those bones and scattered it for all eternity.

Saul examined an abandoned tractor. Its tires were flat and cracked, its seat all wire where once there had been a cushion. One of its headlights drooped. Saul climbed onto the tractor and played with the shift. When he wiped a gauge, he saw the tank was empty—that tractor was another set of bones that would disappear in a hundred years. From that height Saul could see some of his neighborhood. What was his father doing? The fan belt would have been fitted by now, and Saul guessed his father was probably in the house making slipcovers. He could picture in his mind how his father would look up from his handiwork and ask, "Well?"

Three miles from home, Saul figured that he was far enough.

Or was it? How far did you have to go to get rid of a dog? And was it possible? It would forever be a burden in his memory. What if Lucky retraced his footsteps, his smell, and found his way home? His father would be really mad. He would yell at him, and yank the dog into his pickup truck.

"I won't let him," Saul found himself muttering. Saul was determined to do it himself, to do it right.

But he sensed that he had to continue farther. His ankles were sore from walking over clods and dipping into holes. He was hungry. He was mad at himself for not bringing water. Lucky could drink from puddles, but he would have to wait.

They walked on, with Lucky sometimes drifting ahead and other times poking his nose into holes and holding up the progress. The sky was cold but clear. The sun warmed the right side of his face.

"Come on," Saul called when Lucky found another hole, or foolishly tried to run after a rabbit.

Loose-legged, Lucky happily came running when Saul called.

A mile later, Saul bent down and picked up a mud-caked dog collar. He turned it over in his hands. He wondered whether some other boy's father had made him abandon his dog in the country. Or had the dog walked himself out into the field to die? He knew cats were wired for this sort of instinct. If they were sick they would leave, quiet as smoke, and go off to die on their own.

Saul tossed the collar aside—he didn't want anything to do with it, or the snake that approached them. It was slithering sideways, its luminous yellow eyes focused on him. The snake halted, spat out its tongue at them, waved it around, and then moved on.

The sky rolled with clouds, dark underneath but lit on top by the sun. Saul figured that it was going to rain. He walked thinking of his mother, how she was probably returning home from church, or maybe the market. What would they have that evening? There would be beans and rice, but the main dish? The radio would be turned to a Spanish-language station, the television also going loud with a Mexican *telenovela*. Saul would eat because he had to eat, had to be like his father...practical.

Saul walked over soil that was no longer farmland but just hard earth. Tumbleweeds rolled, rabbits jumped and ran. The hardy weeds lived on nothing. When you sprayed the weeds with poisons they came back even angrier, with thorns and stickers. The land was tough.

Finally Saul stopped, though his heart kept moving. The wind seemed to shove him from behind. This was the place for his dog, miles from humans. Saul picked up a stick and turned it over in his hands. It was a splintery stick, and for a second he thought of running his palm against the grain. Slivers would shoot into his skin and shock him with pain.

Instead, he spanked the stick lightly into his palm. It wasn't too heavy. He planned to get a running start, with all his strength of heart and legs, and send it sailing like a javelin. But first he took out a plastic bag of dog food. He would leave it behind, and when Lucky returned with the stick in his mouth he would drop it, sniff the plastic bag, and tear into it.

"Lucky, poor Lucky," he said in a near whimper. "I love you, boy. Dad is mean." He pictured the fall day when Lucky had appeared on their back porch and scratched the door—he was a skinny but happy dog who ran right into his arms when Saul answered that door. That was four years earlier, when he was in fourth grade and struggling in school.

"Bye, Lucky," Saul cried. When he frowned, tears began to roll down his cheeks. He wiped them and looked down: what was the difference between tears and rain? But he knew. Rain was cold and heartless, but tears were salty, alive with passion. "Bye, Lucky," he repeated. "Bye, Lucky." He took three charging steps and hurled the stick.

Lucky, head raised, watched it turn end over end. On

hurt bones Lucky lumbered after the stick, and after he dropped the plastic bag Saul bolted in the other direction. He ran over uneven ground, the slap of his tennis shoes kicking up pads of mud. Head down, he ran as fast and hard as he could. At first there was plenty of air in his lungs, but soon he was gasping. He slowed to a steady jog, but still didn't dare turn around, scared that he might run back to Lucky.

When he passed the tractor he estimated that he was halfway home. He slowed to a walk with sweat in his eyes, and looked back: no Lucky. There was just a landscape of tumbleweeds. A rabbit, gray as clouds, scurried from some brush. A pop of a truck on the road sounded and the faint noise of an airplane buzzed like a gnat. When Saul thought he heard a bark he ran again, but not as fast. He was tired and thirsty, and ashamed of what he had done. He had abandoned Lucky, his old dog who loved him more than anyone else in the world.

He stopped and bent over with his hands on his knees. He could feel that his face was red and sweaty. Wasn't this the worst thing that a boy could do? He pictured his footprints filling with rain, and Lucky whimpering. His dog would drink from the footprints, look up for his boy, and drink again.

Saul, with his lips trembling, turned. The sun was behind a bank of clouds and the wind was blowing across the ground. What was wrong with him? How could he do such a thing to Lucky?

"You can hit me if you want," he imagined muttering to his father, "but Lucky's coming home." He could picture his father's gnashing teeth as he raised a belt to hit him. He didn't care.

"I don't care what you say," Saul said, and started running back to find Lucky. He would run all over that barren farmland, all over the state, to find Lucky. Once he did, he would hug him, cry into his fur, and lift him into his arms. He couldn't wait to let his friend lick his face and show him his deepest tears. What kind of person could abandon such a great friend? Not a person like himself.

Musical Lives

After band practice Joel set off with his trumpet case in one hand and a glazed donut in the other. His friend Matt did the same. They also wore backpacks crammed with books and homework and gym clothes stinking of sweat and defeat. At twelve, life wasn't getting easier for either one of them. School began at dawn when the light was the color of a bruise and ended in bruises.

"What do you think?" Joel asked.

The band teacher, Mr. Franks, had informed the boys that only one trumpeter would make the marching band. He would decide who by next practice, but first he had to decide which student would march in the trombone section. He told the boys, none too quietly, that the trombone section was awful but he had to keep at least three of the musicians, a decision that was making his stomach ache.

"You're better," Matt said.

Joel let this thought roll in his mind. Was he better? The

last three notes he delivered of "The Star-Spangled Banner" imitated duck quacks and would not have stirred even the most patriotic heart. But he also remembered that Matt had stumbled over more notes. Maybe he was better, the result of his mother making him practice in his bedroom, with the door open so that she could keep her eye on him. Still, to his best friend he felt obligated to argue, "No, you're better."

Joel had taken trumpet lessons since he was nine, and now, on the verge of his teenage years (he would be thirteen in two weeks), he realized that he would never be really good at trumpet—or any instrument, including the triangle or the pots and pans he used to bang when he was really little. He had even lost faith that lugging his trumpet case would at least harden his biceps. And his parents! They often made him play for relatives, who would sit on their couch and listen to him blare "When Johnny Comes Marching Home." The wind from his lungs would travel through every nook and cranny of the trumpet before rushing from the bell. It was a struggle. His playing succeeded only in rattling the nerves of their dog, Patches, who joined in, howling!

The two boys, strolling from the school campus, devoured two donuts each and shared a box of Nerds. They smacked their lips and wished for a carton of milk to descend from the sky to wash down all that sugar. Joel had promised to cut down on sweets, as he was conscious of the tsunami of fat that spilled over his waist. But it was difficult, maybe impossible, now that his older brother, a culinary student, kept bringing home leftover baked goods.

They cut a path through the park and stopped at a drinking fountain. They sat on the bench. A cargo of clouds moved above them, taking with them rain and lightning, and the sweet smell that followed a shower.

"You know where I would like to go?" Matt asked his friend.

Joel, lost in thought, was staring at his palms with their dry river of lines. The last time they filled, he was crying over forgetting Mother's Day. The lines filled with tears that he rubbed into his pants when he was all done. "I don't know," Joel answered as he closed his hands into tiny fists. He stretched his arms above his head and said, "I wish I had a soda."

Matt raised his face upward and gazed beyond the trees. "Space. No one would bother me if I was up there." He told Joel how he would have a large spaceship, one big enough for a Ping-Pong table and a couple of friends.

Joel pictured Ping-Pong balls slowly ricocheting off all the instrument panels. He wondered why that was, why things were slow in space—a pencil floating in the space-ship came to mind, and a water bottle with the word NASA printed on its side. Was time slow up in space, too? Would you be young forever up in space? He would hate always being young. He wanted to be grown up and be in the adult world, where bullies were, by then, behind bars in any of California's many prisons.

Joel stopped his daydreaming. He wasn't in space but a park, where the swings and slides were tagged with graffiti. "Yeah, I guess it would be cool," he remarked weakly.

"What's wrong?" Matt asked.

"You know what's wrong," Joel said and stood up. "School and everything." He toed the ground with his shoe and went through his pocket for gum. Finding none, he sat back down. "If I could go anywhere far it would be the North Pole." He laughed and said, "I used to believe in Santa."

"Santa was cool," Matt said, his short legs swinging from the bench. "We were little then. Santa was real." He shook his head at a memory. "But he always just brought me clothes and stuff like this." He kicked the trumpet case.

Joel looked skyward. The clouds were moving in file obediently, he thought, all in a row and filled with rain. Rain was good. Rain cleaned the streets and watered the natural world. It filled lakes and rivers, and made corn grow—these were Joel's thoughts, along with the feeling that he was a loser. He hated himself for eating donuts.

The boys rested before they got up. They didn't get very far before Mark, a classmate, yelled from the basketball court, "Hey, get over here."

"You mean us?" Joel asked, tempted to look around.

Mark was a starter for the school's basketball team and vice president of their seventh-grade class, a position he kept even after he was accused of smoking in the boys' restroom. Matt never knew for sure about that infraction, but he could clearly imagine Mark leaning against a basin with a halo of cigarette smoke floating over his head. He loathed visiting the restroom, where bullies lurked like vampires and the toilets always seemed to run. And if you looked inside one of the toilet bowls . . . he shuddered.

Joel and Matt moved suspiciously toward Mark and Ryan, who were dressed in Golden State jerseys. Their trunks were halfway off their butts. Their shoes seemed too large for their feet.

"What?" Joel asked.

Mark rolled the basketball up and down his arm. He bounced it at his feet and between his feet. "Let's play," Mark said.

The two boys looked at each other. Matt could tell that Joel wanted to bail. He wondered whether his friend was thinking about outer space.

"We're no good," Joel remarked after he swiveled his head toward Mark. He would have felt embarrassed admitting this to a lesser player than Mark and his smirking friend, Ryan. But just as the sun came up in the east and set in the west, it was the truth. He was no good at sports. The last time he played basketball, a kid made layup after layup against him. Why he stood there, hands out as if to tackle him, was a mystery.

"What do you mean?" Mark scolded. "You're good. I seen you play." He turned his face to the ground and smiled.

Liar, Joel thought. He's never seen me do anything. He wouldn't even recognize him in the band while it played for the team at home games.

Ryan grabbed the ball from Mark and dribbled in place for a few seconds before rocketing toward the basket to make an effortless layup. He turned and scolded, "Come on. Don't be chicken."

Don't be chicken!

Joel had learned from his father that insults were meaningless unless you took them to heart.

"We got to go home," Matt said. "We got to practice."

"What, guitar?" Mark asked with a snarl on his face.

"No, the trumpet." Matt answered.

"Oh, 'the trumpet.'" Mark made quotation marks in the air as he repeated, "The trumpet." He laughed and bumped fists with Ryan. Then he repeated his challenge to play and not be chicken.

Joel and Matt again looked at each other, both aware that the court was no place for them. Still, Joel figured that he and Matt could split up—he could play with Ryan, and Matt with Mark. It wouldn't hurt to exercise. Plus, he could later say to his parents, maybe his classmates, that Mark and Ryan let him play with them. Surely his and Joel's status at school would go up a notch.

"Okay, how 'bout Ryan and me?" Joel suggested.

"Nah, man," Mark said with a growl. He tugged up his trunks. "Me and Ryan against you gladiators."

Neither Joel nor Matt stirred. Time slowed, just like time in space. Joel couldn't help but think of a shoot-out in a cowboy movie.

"But that won't be fair," Matt said finally. He was picking up his trumpet from the ground, readying for an exit.

"You guys are way better," Joel said. He could see himself sandwiched between them and roughed up by elbows and swatting palms. And if that didn't make his face squeeze out tears, then certainly their funky-smelling sweat would overwhelm him.

"What do you mean?" Ryan said. He was dribbling the ball between his legs. "Just because we're on the team and you guys..."—he eyed the trumpet cases—"blow horns." He started laughing and stepped over to Mark to slap palms.

"You know it won't be fair," Joel replied.

"We're hurting," Mark claimed. He winced and touched the small of his back. "I'm messed up all over from playing on Sunday."

"I'm messed up, too," Ryan said. But he didn't wince or massage any part of his body. He made the remark as he eyed the hoop—he released the ball, which swished the net.

"Nah, we got to go," Joel said.

"Don't be like that," Mark said. "We'll shoot with our left hands."

Joel and Matt hesitated.

"We'll be like old people," Mark added. "All slow and everything."

Joel looked at Matt. They shrugged and moved their trumpet cases and backpacks to the bench. They returned to the court.

"Let me take a practice shot," Joel said. It had been years since he had made a basketball shot, since fifth grade, when he played two girls in a game of "horse."

Ryan let the basketball roll from his hands and walked away, his untied shoelaces dragging like the tentacles of an octopus.

Joel hustled to pick up the ball. He was surprised by its weight—it was heavy. He bounced it and recalled—it was a painful image—how only two years ago he used both hands to dribble. He wasn't an athlete then and wasn't one now. Still, he had to save face. In the presence of Mark and Ryan, he made the effort to keep the ball bouncing with only one hand. He took a step, his eyes on the ball, stopped under the shadow of the backboard, and raised his face to the hoop. He was surprised how high the hoop was. Still, he lifted the basketball, aimed, and shot it in the direction of the hoop. He "bricked."

Matt took a few shots, but he was just as bad.

"Come on, you guys are warmed up," Mark said. "We take out."

"Don't we shoot for take-outs?" Joel asked.

"Not here," Mark said. "You're the visitors." He quickly

passed the ball to Ryan, who took it in for an easy layup. The net swished like a Hawaiian skirt.

"Two nothing," Ryan barked. He hustled to the top of the key and shot the ball to Mark, who weaved between Joel and Matt and did a layup.

"Four *nada*," Mark muttered. He took the ball out, passing it to Ryan, who, bent over, dribbled in front of Joel, daring him, "Come on—get it!"

"You said you were going to play with your left hand," Joel said.

"That's right, huh," Ryan said. "But I lied." He clipped Joel's shoulder as he drove to the basket. When he missed a layup, Joel scrambled for the ball. But Mark pushed him from behind, grabbed the ball, aimed standing like a stork on one leg, and made his shot.

Matt put his hands on his hips. "This isn't fair."

"What's not fair? You a dude, ain't you?" Mark remarked. "This is basketball." He tossed the ball to Joel and said, "We'll be nice. You guys take out."

Steaming, Joel dribbled the ball as he walked to the edge of the court. He wished they hadn't walked through the park, or hadn't gone to school at all. Most of all, he wished Mark and Ryan would trip over their untied shoelaces.

When Joel tossed the ball to Matt, who was waiting with both hands out, Ryan swooped and intercepted it. He tossed it to Mark, who circled the court, the ball sometimes bouncing between his legs and other times spanking the ground like a paddle ball. Ryan finally made a screen and Mark went up for a layup.

"Six nothing," Mark announced. Then it was eight nothing, then ten nothing...

"They're good, huh?" Mark asked Ryan, who said, "You guys haven't started yet. You'll probably catch us real soon."

By the time it was fourteen to zero, Mark and Ryan played dirty, elbowing first Joel and then Matt. When the score was eighteen to zero, Ryan bounced the ball against Joel's face and bloodied his lip.

"Aw, I'm sorry," Ryan moaned. "It slipped."

Joel bent over, cupping his mouth. He looked at his palm: a smear of blood. He stood up, his eyes misted, and said, "You did that on purpose."

"Nah, I didn't. I told you it slipped."

"We got to go," Joel said through his bruised mouth.

"The game ain't over," Mark said angrily. "And you owe us."

Joel made the mistake of asking what he and Joel owed them.

"Five dollars," Ryan answered for Mark. "That's what we bet."

"We didn't make a bet," Matt argued.

But that didn't stop Ryan from grabbing Matt from behind and pushing his hand into his pocket. He drew out a packet of gum, his comb, a pen, and thirty-five cents.

Matt struggled to break free, which was a mistake because he elbowed Ryan, who let out a small cry of pain. Ryan let go and backed up a few steps. He gathered himself and then punched Matt in the face.

Matt backpedaled on his heels, both hands cupping his mouth. He looked at his palms.

"That slipped, too," Ryan barked.

"You guys are bullies," Joel cried under his breath. "You guys ain't that good."

"What did you say?" Mark said, his fists closed as he approached Joel. "I should smack you again. You guys are weak." He swiveled away like a boxer, swearing that if he weren't the vice president of the class he would get him in a headlock and ram his head into the tetherball pole.

"Right on," Ryan chimed in. He bumped fists with Mark.

Joel and Matt picked up their trumpets and backpacks, not bothering to answer the taunts. They dragged themselves to the drinking fountain. There they washed their faces and slurped gingerly, as their mouths were now puffy.

"I wish I was Harry Potter," Joel moaned. He told Matt how he would fly and dunk the balls one after another, and taunt Mark and Ryan.

"Harry Potter?" Matt asked. "He ain't real, either. He's like Santa Claus. It's all make-believe."

The two boys walked away from the park. Leaves were falling and the sun, too, seemed to have fallen behind the roofs. In an hour it would be dark and the lawns wet from dew. The day began bruise-dark and was now ending with bruised faces.

"I hate them," Matt said with a whine in his voice.

"Me, too," Joel said as he touched his lip. He was done with music. There was nothing to play that would make him happy. And for sure—if Mr. Franks chose him over Matt—he would refuse to play for the school band. No, he wouldn't do it! He wasn't about to play the trumpet for a basketball team with players like Mark and Ryan. He could tell Mr. Franks that he quit, that his lips were bruised and tender.

Let his trumpet sit in the hall closet, next to the vacuum cleaner, his kind of musical instrument. When you plugged it in and hit the switch, it, too, howled with something like pain.

A Very Short Romance

When my friend Hannah said, "Go ahead, kiss him," I turned around, blushed, twirled in a circle one way, then another, and kissed the back of my hand. I was afraid, like that time on a dare I jumped off of my dog's doghouse. I closed my eyes and felt really strange jumping, and all the while Valentine, my dog, was looking at me.

"Come on, don't be chicken," Hannah cried in happiness.

I felt like collapsing on the school lawn and letting Mr. Olds, the janitor, rake leaves around me and bury me for good. I was giddy, weak-kneed. I was happy about something, and not necessarily from liking a certain boy.

"Danny likes you, I know he does," Hannah screamed, and plopped onto the grass.

Danny was a boy in biology, math, and English. He was short, super smart, and (I thought) awfully cute. So what if his pants were short? So what if his socks were ducky white? So what that he had a Batman backpack, that he combed his hair with a part on the side, that he tucked a paper napkin in the front of his shirt when he ate lunch?

"He's a frog," Hannah said as she sat on the lawn. "Kiss him and he'll turn into a prince."

"Shut up already," I cried, and threw a handful of leaves at her. I plopped right down next to my giggling friend.

"He plays guitar," Hannah said, unhooking a leaf from her hair. "He'll write you a song."

"Get out!"

"He loves you," Hannah teased.

"Stop it," I said. But I didn't want her to stop it. I liked it, I liked it a lot.

Hannah held a large leaf like a fan against her face. Behind this leaf she said, "I'll give you a hundred dollars if you do it."

"You lie," I answered. "You don't have any money."

"I do," Hannah said, with eyes wide in shock that I didn't believe her. She pointed to the tree we sat under. "I have more money than that tree has leaves." She fell onto her back and said that she would like to go to the moon, or if not the moon then maybe a star where she could look down at our school and say, "Hey, everybody, I'm up here."

We had just taken a math test and were glad that that was over. I might have gotten the answer to how long it would take a train traveling 50 miles an hour to reach Rochester, New York. The distance was 832 miles.

Where in the world was Rochester, anyway? It didn't matter.

What mattered was Hannah and me on the lawn after school. It was October, cool but not cold yet, and the leaves were burnt orange, really pretty. In a month the trees would be bare and we wouldn't be able to sit on the lawn or any other lawn. We would be huddled in sweaters and jackets, with our faces red from the cold.

Hannah rolled onto her stomach, pushed herself up to sitting position, and ripped a large leaf in half.

"This is your heart," Hannah remarked.

"What?" I asked.

"It's going to tear down the middle because years and years from now you're going to realize you missed your chance." Her face was serious.

"You mean about kissing Danny?"

Hannah nodded her head. "He's in love with you."

I could tell she was struggling to contain that smile just beneath the layer of pretty teeth—and she was pretty, a girl with large eyes and the pouting mouth of a teen model. I was pretty, too, with twinkling eyes and a mouth like a valentine.

"Let me have it," I said, and grabbed the torn leaf from her hand. I looked at the two halves, like parts of a sewing pattern that I tried to piece together. "This is my heart?"

Pouting, she nodded. "Poor heart."

I had to laugh and crumble the heart into confetti pieces. I turned my attention to the front of our school. Mr. Olds was lowering the flag. The sun was sinking and a chill was beginning. I don't know why, but maybe because I was so happy it was Friday, I said, "Hannah, I'll kiss the next boy who comes out of the front doors."

"You promise!" she nearly screamed.

I crossed my heart.

We watched the front door. A girl came out—Sarah someone—and two adults, parents, we guessed. Two more girls came out, but with a boy. We decided that it had to be a boy alone, not a boy with others.

Then I tore the leaf that I was holding into more pieces when Danny, his white socks showing below his high-water pants, appeared from the front door.

"No," I screamed. "No, no, no!" Of all people!

Hannah fell backward, laughing. She told me I was going to marry him, and I told her I wasn't going to marry anyone with socks like his!

When Hannah sat back up, I fell backward. The sky was blue and so high. It seemed to go on and on, just like school. Maybe somewhere far away, on another planet where there was air and water and trees and love, some other girl like me was sitting with her best friend.

"You promised," Hannah said. "Kiss him. He's your frog!"

I sat back up, got to my feet, told Hannah to stop laughing, and marched over to Danny, who was unlocking his bike.

"Danny," I called.

Danny turned.

"Danny, I have something to give you." Wasn't kissing sort of a gift?

Danny let his bike chain fall with a clang.

"Are you a frog?" I asked in a near whisper as I stood so close that we were almost touching.

"What?"

"Don't you like me?" I continued.

Danny took a step back. "What do you mean?"

"I mean you're cute." I saw that he had a packet of Kleenex in his shirt pocket. Could anyone be so sweet! And cute, with his shirt buttoned all the way up, and his hair tangled by something deep inside his smart, smart brain!

"I can't do that," Danny said as my face approached his.

"Why?"

"Because..."

At that moment a girl came hurrying down the steps, her dress dancing about her knees. She held a candy bar in her hand, and her face was almost glowing. She offered the candy bar to Danny's mouth, but he stepped away, then stepped toward it. He took it from her hands (they were so tiny) and took a bite.

Like shame! Like what a fool I was!

I turned and saw Hannah, whose smile had disappeared. She had teased me to get Danny, that nerd with a Batman backpack, to kiss me.

But Danny, the goof, already had a girlfriend, and just think, there I was throwing myself at him! Danny and the girl rode off on his bike, she balanced on the bar and he struggling to keep it going, on a Friday afternoon in October. The leaves were falling, brilliant red, but not as red as my cheeks.

Finding Religion

The fact was Cynthia Rodriguez had no problem with ladling gravy over a mound of rice. True, it was work. Steam wet her face, rouged her cheeks, and made her appetite disappear, though that particular morning she had eaten only a muffin before she slid into the family van for the short drive to St. Anthony's Soup Kitchen. She volunteered every other Saturday because her father expected—no, demanded—that *his* daughter go to college. He believed that working in the soup kitchen would help her get into college. Schools were looking for young people who help others.

That was her father's strategy, but Cynthia did volunteer work for other reasons. She felt sad for people without enough to eat or a place to stay. She didn't mind if her feet hurt for a couple of hours or that her wrists gave way. She didn't mind that she had to chop carrots, celery, and onions, the last forcing tears from her eyes.

She didn't mind that her friends were playing soccer at that hour, or that others were still in pajamas in front of their computers. It always saddened her that the line of homeless extended out the door. Was the world that hungry?

But this Saturday was unusual. In line and advancing slowly toward her position was her classmate Alma Silva, a girl she hardly knew. Alma wore a cap to her ears. She was bundled in a jacket that reached to her knees.

It occurred to Cynthia that Alma was trying to hide. She felt for her classmate. She located a new feeling near her heart, a feeling that had no word.

"Hi," said Cynthia. She had decided not to add "Alma" to her greeting because she wished her friend to remain anonymous.

"Hi," Alma answered in kind.

That was it.

Alma moved away with her plate and joined a woman who must have been her mother. The mother was wearing a hat and a large jacket.

Cynthia thought about this chance meeting with Alma, and at dinner that night she had only one helping of green enchiladas.

"You're not hungry, *mi'ja?*" her mother asked as she rose for seconds. Her napkin fell like a large snowflake from her lap.

"No, I'm fine," Cynthia answered. She retrieved the napkin and placed it on her mother's chair. All during dinner she wanted to tell her parents about Alma. At last she said, "Today at the kitchen I saw someone from school."

"She's volunteering there?" her mother asked at the stove. She let out a small "ouch" from picking up the ladle to add sauce to her enchilada.

"No," Cynthia answered. She turned to her father across the table and said, "She eats there." She looked him in his eyes and searched for a response.

She eats there.

"This girl...eats there?" he asked. He himself had a fork piled with rice. He lowered the fork a few inches as he became interested.

"Yesterday she was there. I've never seen her before."

"You know her?" he probed

"No, not really. She's a girl from school."

Her father's attention turned to a jogger passing their large dining room window. He lowered his gaze—What is he thinking? Cynthia wondered—and then brought the forkful of rice to his mouth. Right then, Cynthia promised herself that she would try eating the food at St. Anthony's—just to see, just to taste something new.

Later, in her bedroom, Cynthia took out three of her thirteen My Little Ponies and placed them on her chest of drawers. She was twelve and really too old to play with them. She imagined that the ponies needed air and exercise, and though she knew it was babyish she galloped them across the field of her bed. After she tired of this play, she lay on her bed and evaluated her parents' situation. She was proud of them, as they both worked hard and provided her with lots of things. But their response to Alma was confusing. Did they fear her? Were they worried that *their* daughter might become friends with a poor girl?

On Monday morning she woke to her stomach growling from hunger. For breakfast she made an egg burrito for herself. She walked the three blocks to school, kicking through leaves and righting a garbage can that a dog—or was it a person?—had knocked over. The half crowns of eggshells reminded her of her egg burrito, and she rubbed her stomach. I'm fed, she thought, and I'm okay.

At school Cynthia recalled a catechism story about how Jesus had fasted for what . . . forty days? Or was it that it rained forty days? No matter, Jesus was very skinny, or so Cynthia assumed from all the images she saw of him. Jesus knew hunger, and he knew thirst. He converted water into wine and healed with his touch. He was a person who helped people and indirectly provided the poor with bread. He also provided them with faith, which for her was so strong that you could stand your ground against bullies and mean people. She knew that wasn't true faith, but closer than two years ago when she thought faith meant going to heaven after years and years of going to church. She went to church only once a month, usually with her mother.

"You need a little religion," Cynthia remembered her mother saying. *A little religion*. It was like her father requiring her to volunteer every other weekend. She just needed a little, not a lot.

Cynthia could trace her sympathy for the poor. She was six years old and playing in the front yard of their old house when two foster children living next door had to move. They departed with their personal items in garbage bags. They feel like garbage, she remembered thinking, but they're not. She was scared for them, and scared for herself as she began to understand that it was possible that her own father might get hurt at work (at the time, he was the person who scaled telephone poles). Then what would happen to her? That day she became aware how fragile life was, like a flower, like a bird's egg. She felt weak. The foster children got into cars and disappeared without returning her wave of good-bye.

At school Cynthia searched out Alma and found her bending over a drinking fountain. When Alma turned and spied Cynthia, her eyes immediately looked down the hallway.

"Hi, Alma," Cynthia started to say, but the girl fled.

The day was unpleasant. In biology Cynthia was given a small knife to probe a frog in a white pan. She and others squealed at cutting into frogs and seeing for themselves the heart, the stomach, and the sinews that made frogs jump. She turned the knife the wrong way and sawed the frog. She couldn't help but think that it was like playing a very small cello.

Later Cynthia walked home, troubled. She didn't want anyone to have to stand in line for their food. Why couldn't people just show up at tables and the plates of food would be there, steaming? And why couldn't people just take what they needed? Their own house had only three bedrooms, with two baths, and the yard had lemon and apple trees. This wasn't too much, was it? But she noticed that the vehicles passing were large SUVs and an occasional Hummer. Couldn't people just walk? Why couldn't they plant a small tree on the side of a barren mountain and sing, "O tree, grow to be mighty"?

But instead of returning home, Cynthia had a strong urge to do something good—right then! If only everyone did something good, she mused, the world wouldn't be so messed up. People would start being nice. Gangs would remove their tattoos and get jobs. There would be no wars.

She visited the unpaved canal hoping that maybe she could water a small tree growing on its banks. It might be thirsty, she figured, and need a little water to survive. She wanted to be useful, to be kind to something, to do something more than ladle gravy onto rice. At the canal she slowed to a stop when she came upon two middle school boys. Smoke rose from their mouths when their lips parted.

They're not supposed to be smoking, she thought as she continued down the side of the canal, far from the boys and the rush of cars on Main Street. She was searching for something good to do, something that would bring her face-to-face with a good deed. Why did she have to wait to do a good deed every other Saturday, when it could happen every day of your life?

Cynthia found only rugged bushes with litter attached to their spiky branches. There was also debris—a mattress, car tires, cans, and broken bottles. The carcass of a stripped bike lay abandoned in the stagnant water.

"It's ugly," she lamented. "I wish God would come and stop it."

She made out the sound of a frog and stepped lightly along the bank. She parted tall weeds and there it was— the last surviving frog? It's not a pretty thing, she admitted, but still a live creature.

"Poor thing," she muttered. She pictured all of the other frogs at school, their tiny frog arms pointing up, pointing at her and her classmates. The dead frogs were accusing them of something.

Cynthia paused when she noticed a flattened plastic garbage bag on the bank. She recalled the foster children. Her mind imagined the children being driven away and deposited at the canal, where they lived among feral cats, slithering salamanders and snakes, and the last of the frogs before they were gathered up for biology students— dead. Perhaps the foster children ended up homeless, hunkered around small campfires. The end of the plastic garbage bag fluttered, then became still.

Later that evening her mother appeared disenchanted when Cynthia raised the question of whether Alma was homeless. Her voice became edgy when she answered, "No, of course she has a home. All girls her age have homes."

Cynthia didn't pursue the issue. She worked on her homework for a few minutes, and then gathered her things and went to her bedroom. She thought: If I knew Alma's dad or mom's first name, I could look up in the phonebook and call the number to see if she lives there. She then dreamily imagined Alma staying with her. After all, she had a large bed. She could place a row of My Little Ponies to divide the bed. Wouldn't that be cute?

At school the next day, Cynthia saw Alma come out of the cafeteria. Her arm was locked in another girl's arm, and they were happy. But Alma's happiness collapsed when she saw Cynthia.

"Hi," Cynthia called out in a friendly way, and Alma returned her greeting with a "Hi." But there was nothing behind it, no feeling. Yet after they passed Cynthia heard Alma's laughter return. Right then Cynthia figured that Alma was not as troubled as she believed, just embarrassed at being seen at the soup kitchen. After all, Alma had a good friend and her spirit was happy—or else why the laughter?

Alma is going to go one way, and I'm going another, Cynthia concluded.

But Cynthia was determined to see for herself what it felt like standing in line and being served. On Saturday she asked her father to drive her to St. Anthony's, and he obliged because he had to go the hardware store.

"I'll be back in two hours," he said after he walked her inside. "But let's not make this a habit."

"What?" she asked.

"Helping," he answered.

After her father drove away she found something to do. She scraped plates and took out bags of garbage to the Dumpster. She hurled them almost angrily as she recalled the foster children. What had her father said? Not make a habit of helping?

Since Cynthia was relegated to the back, she wasn't certain if Alma came that day. But she was certain the line was long, possibly longer than last Saturday, and there were girls her age and some younger.

The poor will always be with us. She remembered that from somewhere. But so will parents, she argued. She loved hers, but sometimes they said things that confused her. Wasn't she meant to help make the world better?

When she finished her jobs, Cynthia helped herself to a plate of food—spaghetti that was only medium warm. She found herself at a table near a man with a sore on his lip. She picked up a large spoon—dented, she noticed, by teeth marks. It felt a little strange, but she wanted to know how it felt to sit with the homeless. She prayed that the person coming through the door would be a friend, a classmate, a relative, someone like herself—and that this person would come soon. With a hard bun broken in half, she was ready to eat.

Celebrities

On Monday and Tuesday Laura was Katy Perry, the sweetest rocker since the beginning of time, and learned all the lyrics from her second smash CD. She bounced around her bedroom and screamed the songs until her throat was so hoarse that she had to go into seclusion on Wednesday. From Thursday through Saturday Laura became Taylor Swift, the country star, and wore a cowboy hat her parents bought for her at the Fresno District Fair when she was six. Then for an hour or two Laura became Amy Winehouse, mascara and all, and even tossed her head as she imagined Amy Winehouse might do onstage—or in jail. Her mother had scolded, "That looks cheap."

"But Mom," Laura argued, "do you know much it costs to do cheap?" The mascara and eyeliner had cost nineteen dollars, not to mention the fishnet stockings she could wear only in her bedroom—those were six dollars at Cheapo Katie's in a cheapo strip mall by the fairgrounds.

If her mother ever found them, she would take a pair of scissors and snip them into black dental floss.

But Sunday Laura decided that she wanted to be Miley Cryus, and began to learn her songs in the bedroom of her best friend, Jasmine, who herself decided to become Alexis, a girl singer she had read about in *People* magazine. Alexis was Greek, and was famous there, in Greece, and super rich—or how could she afford the yacht where she stood, hips pushed out, with a super good-looking guy at her side? Alexis sported sunglasses on top of her head, the universal sign that the babe was rich. Plus, her shark-like teeth revealed a personality that said she wanted a big bite of the world.

"He's super hot!" Jasmine reported, and brought her painted fingernails to her mouth. She squealed.

"Let me see," Laura said, and grabbed the magazine from Jasmine. Within two or three bats of her heavily mascaraed lashes, she realized her friend was right. He was cute, cute, cute! Laura burned a hole in the image of this hunk with a stomach dimpled with muscles. His belly button was staring right at her.

"But you can have him," Jasmine said. "His hair's all curly. I like boys with straight hair."

"Nah, I'm going to remain faithful. What if Kevin found out?"

Kevin was the Kevin of the Jonas Brothers. Laura had dated him in her mind, and done more than that after she bought his poster. She had placed the lightest of light kisses on his mouth, and giggled when she went all out by placing lipstick-smeared smooches on both of his cheeks. Near the bottom of the poster she had written in purple ink, "To my Darling Laura. Lov Ya! Kevin." She then spiffed it up by adding little dancing hearts.

"Kevin won't care," Jasmine argued. "Joe says that Kevin has an open mind."

Joe was the Joe of the Jonas Brothers, the most famous group since the beginning of the world as far as the girls knew. He was Jasmine's boyfriend.

Both girls had fantasy-dated two of the three Jonas brothers. They felt sorry for Nick, the youngest Jonas Brother, but they figured in time he would find someone, even if that someone had to be Jasmine's little sister, Cheryl. Cheryl was in fifth grade, but by the time she was in seventh grade, the grade they would enter in the fall, she would be ready for Nick. By then Nick would have grown tired of all the girls in the world, and the only one left would be Cheryl.

The girls laughed.

"Can you imagine Joe with Cheryl?"

Only an hour earlier they had seen Cheryl at the curb chomping on a Popsicle. The corners of her mouth were stained red, and her left knee was red with a fresh scab from falling off a skateboard.

Laura and Jasmine threw themselves on the bed, disturbing a herd of stuffed animals, mostly unicorns and palomino horses. Laura herself had stuffed animals lined up on her bed and two American Girl dolls *under* the bed—Josefina and Marisol—in casket-like boxes forever in the dark. When Laura was alone, her iPod thumping music into her not-yet-pierced ears, she would sometimes comb the mane of her favorite unicorn, Princess. She would comb Princess's mane and feel only slightly babyish when she peered at the poster of Kevin smiling down on her among her rain of purple hearts. She wondered whether Kevin played with his old toys, or did he give them away to charity?

"Come on." Jasmine beckoned to Laura. "Let's go outside."

They bounced off the bed. Before they left they took off most of their mascara, but replenished their lips with loads of lipstick. They exited the bedroom as themselves, Laura and Jasmine, because it wasn't worth the effort playing someone famous in front of anyone's parents. Why bother? Their parents were old and, like wow, born in the last century! They were so glad that they had been born in 2000, a great year.

Sure enough, Jasmine's parents were watching the news on television. They swiveled their heads toward the two girls, then swiveled them back when a commercial began to show a monster truck crawling up the back of a poor old Volkswagen Beetle. Some kind of car show was coming to the Fresno District Fair.

"I don't know why they do that," Jasmine said under her breath after they skipped through the living room and escaped through the front door.

"Do what?"

"Watch the news. It's just changes."

On the front porch the girls returned to their alter egos, Miley and Alexis. They brought pretend microphones to their mouths, danced looking at their feet, and sang, "I loved him...for a while, just a little while." They bent over in laughter when they couldn't come up with any additional lyrics.

"We sound stupid," Jasmine giggled.

"Yeah, we do," Laura agreed, nearly choking on her gum. She coughed and spit the gum into the flower bed.

"What if Kevin saw you do that?" Jasmine asked, pointing at the gum, which hit a rose petal and disappeared in a clump of weeds.

"Yeah, but what if he saw you like throw up?" She opened her mouth, shot out her neck, and made a retching sound.

"I didn't throw up," Jasmine barked, then laughed. "I only do that when I'm alone."

"Yeah, you did. Remember in second grade?"

Jasmine waved Laura off and said: "I was little then. That was before me and Nick became an item." She hooked her two pinkies together.

They held on to the porch railing, their bodies rocking from laughter. For a second Laura pretended that she was on a yacht. She gazed out on what she imagined was a blue sea with dolphins leaping. In this sea there was a small island with a palm tree. But Laura couldn't build on this vision. What she actually faced was a lawn yellow in areas where the sprinklers were broken. A poorly planted tree was hunched over like a tired old man. If only I had a pair of sunglasses, she thought. And a boyfriend! If only some of it were true.

"Let's go to the mall," Laura suggested when she was drawn from her dream by the sighting of Cheryl, who was hurrying across the street with a Popsicle stick in her mouth.

With Fashion Fair Mall just two blocks away, they didn't even have to cross a busy street. No, they would walk down a tree-lined street and be there in minutes, grateful for the air conditioning and the busyness of shoppers.

"Hi, Cheryl," Laura sang.

Cheryl ran past the two girls without a greeting. She disappeared into the house, her flip-flops flying off her dirty feet.

"Nick will never like her," Jasmine said. "I bet she has to go to the bathroom."

"He will, girl," Laura said in defense of Cheryl. "She's only a little brat now. I bet Nick was a brat when he was her age."

Jasmine was looking at the face of her cell—no calls. "Yeah, I can tell by his smirk that he was a brat." She stuffed the cell into her back pocket. "There's nothing to do."

"Yeah, there is."

"What?"

Laura raised her head and jerked her chin. "The mall," Laura whispered.

"We've been there already," Jasmine whined as she sat on the steps. "We've been there like a thousand times this week. It's stupid."

"Come on," Laura begged. "We can practice being celebrities."

Jasmine clicked her tongue. "I don't know. No one knows Alexis. You at least get to be Miley."

"But Alexis has a yacht and that hunk." She waved her hand in front of her face to indicate that guy was hot. "She was in *People* magazine."

Jasmine stood up, dusting her bottom, and agreed that it wouldn't hurt to circle the mall just once more—they had already been there twice during the day and had witnessed cops escorting a shoplifter through the glass doors. Maybe something worse would happen. Maybe a wall would fall down and they could witness it and say to a television crew, "Like me and my best girl were just walking when like check it out, the wall is really messed up. 'Watch out!' I screamed." They would use their real names, not their celebrity names, so people would recognize them for who they were.

These were Laura's dreams on a summer evening. The

sky was pale, drained of its bluish color. The horizon was orange where the sun was dipping into another world, another time zone. Somewhere down the street a mower started up, failed, and started up again. Somewhere a boy was calling, "I got it."

"It's so nice here," Laura remarked.

"Nice and boring," Jasmine replied.

Laura liked Jasmine's street better than her own. Her neighborhood was the same, really, but some of the neighbors parked their squeaky trucks on the lawn, had loud parties, and stole stuff from each other. Laura's street was kind of like Forever 21 and Jasmine's street was more like Hollister—just nicer.

They were in the driveway when the front door opened and her mother appeared.

"Girls!" she called.

The two turned, like singers.

"Yes?" Jasmine asked in a sultry voice, one shoulder dipped the way she had seen singers do. She pushed up the strap of her bra.

"Where are you two going?"

"To the top, Mom," Jasmine answered. "We're going to chart!"

The girls giggled.

Jasmine's mother didn't pick up that they were now rockers—Miley Cyrus and Alexis, the Greek girl—or that they were not just "girls," but celebrities. This was what Laura was thinking. A small laugh almost erupted, a laugh directed not at Jasmine's mother but at herself. She and Jasmine were just too, too silly. But at age thirteen, what else was there to do?

Jasmine turned to Laura, and Laura, a smirk building up, batted her eyes at Jasmine's mother. The smirk disappeared. She made her mouth small, as if she were pouting.

"To the mall," Laura answered in an almost baby voice.

"To get a soda, Mom," Jasmine breathed huskily. "We'll be right back."

Jasmine's mother approached the girls and narrowed suspicious eyes at them.

"Are you wearing lipstick? And mascara! You look like no-good girls."

Laura and Jasmine automatically sucked in their lips, thus erasing some but not all of the lipstick.

"Is that my perfume?" Jasmine's mother asked. Her nostrils flared as she appraised the scent.

"No, it's mine, Mrs. Gonzalez," Laura answered, bringing her hand over her heart. "It's called Whimsy."

Mrs. Gonzalez bit her lower lip and repeated under her breath, "Whimsy."

"It's Miley's favorite," Jasmine announced.

"Miley," Jasmine's mother repeated dimly. Then she brightened and said, "Oh, her."

"Oh, her!" Jasmine repeated, her hands coming to her hips and, like a gunslinger, legs widening their stance in defiance. "She's a celebrity, Mom. She's like huge." She spread out her arms to make her point.

"That's right," Laura chimed in. "She's famous and nice." She thought of all the people on the television news and how their faces appeared but disappeared within seconds. Not so with Miley. She's *immortal*, a word she learned in sixth grade, which to her understanding meant something permanent, like rocks or the ocean, or gods. Yes, Miley is a goddess, like what's-her-name rising from the sea.

"You girls," Mrs. Gonzalez sighed. She turned without a word and, in pink slippers, went back inside, but not without first warning the girls that they had to be back by eight. The porch light would be on for them.

The mall was dead. The few shoppers roaming the mall seemed to drag their purchases as if they were hauling barbells, not dainty summer outfits. There were no smiles on their faces, just a shine that suggested that shopping was work. Even the balloons at the Hollister store lay on the ground, gasping for air. In the Nike shoe store two salespeople were playing catch with a large sneaker. Two old men with the eyes of sad mules sat on a bench reading newspapers. Now and then they looked up to watch the guy at a food cart twirl pretzels on a finger.

"Miley, this is, like, a cemetery," Jasmine said as she pulled on a length of red whip. She broke off a length and folded it into her mouth.

"This is like the saddest mall, Alexis," Laura agreed. "It's worse than when we went to Olivia Moore's birthday party. Remember?" She recalled the pony Olivia's father had rented that just lay down and wouldn't get up. She sipped her soda, cheeks collapsing on the inhale. She smacked her lips and rattled the ice.

"Poor pony," Jasmine mumbled through her chewing. "I remember its name was Happy."

Laura looked at her friend, ignoring the history of the party pony. "Do you think she's famous—Alexis?"

"She's in *People* magazine."

"But we've never heard a song by that girl. Where's Greece, anyway?"

Jasmine took the soda from Laura and inhaled a tremendous amount of the brownish liquid. She pounded her chest, burped a hearty burp, coughed, and through half-closed eyes exclaimed, "That's cold. Excuse me." She batted her eyelashes and said, "Alexis is not as famous as Miley—no one is, except maybe the pope, who lives near Greece, I think. But the pope doesn't sing, and he can't like girls." She added that she wanted to be famous but not too famous, because famous people, she said, were always having to wake up in the middle of the night to answer the telephone from other famous people. Jasmine was beginning to say that famous people always had to pretend to be happy, unless they were in drug rehabilitation, then it was okay to look like you'd never slept in a million years, when Laura nudged her friend. "Shut up now."

"What?" Her voice was raised a notch. She immediately

began to search for what her friend told her to shut up about.

"See 'em? Be cool." Her eyes slid slowly to two boys in front of Urban Outfitters. The one with blond hair was taller than the one with a Coldplay T-shirt. To Laura they seemed like they were in middle school, like them, but maybe going into high school. In either case they were a new presence, and this ramped up the evening for her and Jasmine.

"Let me see if they be cute," Jasmine said, standing on tiptoes and looking over Laura's shoulder.

"Don't," Laura scolded in a near whisper, hooked her arm in Jasmine's, and led her friend away. This was too exciting. She had the feeling that someone—one of those boys?—was staring at her hips, no, her bottom!

The two sauntered to the entrance of JCPenney and then circled back, stopping once to stare at the summer sale clothes in the window of Macy's. Laura was crazy over the white blouse with a tassel drawstring, and was going to tell Jasmine that it was super, super cute, maybe even affordable, when she saw the boys through the reflection in the glass. Blond Boy was on his cell and Coldplay was just staring—at them!

"Hurry, let's go," Laura whispered, and pulled on Jasmine, who had started to blare that the cream-colored sandals with bows were to die for.

They entered the perfumery, Euphoria, not daring to

gaze back at the boys, who, it seemed to Laura, were trolling for girls. The place was lit up brighter than Disneyland. A poster of a pair of lips—famous lips? Laura wondered— hung on the far wall. From that distance Laura thought they looked okay, but as she strolled in their direction they became like two slugs lying on top of each other— hideously moist. Laura grimaced. She said, "Are those famous?"

"What?" Jasmine bawled. She was shaking a bottle of nail polish.

"Those lips," she said, and pointed.

Jasmine moved her own lips, as if she were eating food. "Katy's? Do I look like Katy?"

I want to be Katy Perry! Laura thought.

"Maybe Demi Henderson," Jasmine guessed a second time. "Those are gigantic lips."

Laura and Jasmine pursed their lips at each other, laughed, and hugged each other when they pointed at the poster of done-up eyes. Jasmine said, "I'd like to have large eyes, but those suckers are too huge. They be big as dartboards!" She made a comment about the cost of keeping those eyes done up in mascara and eyeliner. It would be hecka expensive.

But the laughter diminished when the two boys entered Euphoria and stood momentarily examining a glossy cosmetic purse. Coldplay raised the purse into his arms like a baby and rocked it slowly, then furiously. His friend, Blond Boy, shoved Coldplay, and they left with their hands jammed into their back pockets. But first they cast their eyes at the girls. Laura could have sworn that Blond Boy had pinched his lips up in a sort of a kiss. The boy was bad!

"They're following us," Laura remarked. "I think the blond dude threw me a kiss."

"Did you throw one back?"

"No," Laura sang with a cringe. "I'm not cheap!"

The girls shoved each other playfully and crept behind a display of L'Oréal, products for older women. Laura could feel her heart beat, and would have sworn that the front of her tank top was going up and down.

"Are they still there?" Laura murmured, a small hand mirror raised as she tried to see them from that angle.

Jasmine turned around. "Nah, they gone." She picked up a bottle of perfume. She sniffed it like a bloodhound and said, "It smells like old ladies."

Laura slapped her friend's arm. "That's like rude."

"What?"

"Saying, 'like old ladies.'"

Laura could remember when she first met Jasmine. In second grade Jasmine was loud as the boys—no, louder—and was not above pushing them around to get her way. Seven years later she was still the same.

Laura sighed and turned to the eyeliner in the display. She picked up a turquoise-colored liner and undid the lid. She made a check mark on her wrist, and then another check mark. She peered in the small mirror on the display, and focused in on a mole over her left eyebrow. For years she thought it was ugly, but now with her bangs it was hidden.

"How do I look?" Jasmine asked. She had a large cosmetic bag over one shoulder and was blowing a kiss.

"Alexis, darling," Laura began. It was true, too. She thought the bag looked adorable on Jasmine. If only they could afford it.

They left the store after the assistant manager hurried over in tall heels and asked if she could be of assistance. With her bracelets jangling, she replaced the eyeliners the girls had taken from the stack and stared at the cosmetic bag until Jasmine put it back on the rack.

Laura's anger flared at the thought that the assistant manager—Lauren Whatever, from her nameplate—wanted them out of the store. Sure, they couldn't afford anything, not even the old-lady stuff that was half off, but still, they were customers! Peeved, Laura decided that when she had serious money, loads of it stuffed in every nook and cranny of her Prada purse, she would never shop there. Then she reflected: No, instead of dirty cash, I'll have three gold credit cards. I'll shop there when I'm really rich, and buy everything! I'll bring two Prada purses and stuff them to the gills! I'll show Lauren Whatever!

Once out the door of Euphoria they glided past BCBG, stopping to ogle the clothes on display. They were about to choose outfits that were the sweetest—Laura was determined that the red hoodie would be all the rage—when they heard an echoing "Hey." The "hey" was repeated, and for a moment she wondered, "Is it music from the speakers?"

But it wasn't music, or the start of a song that would lead to dancing. That flat-sounding "hey" belonged to the trolling boys.

Laura turned first, and then Jasmine. They both took a step back, pressing their backs against the glass.

"Hi," the Coldplay guy said after he closed in on the girls.

The blond boy smiled, hands in his back pockets and nodding his head.

"Hi," Laura said with sweetness to her voice. She looked around nervously, pushed herself away from the glass, and remarked, "This place is like dead."

The boys nodded their heads.

"Are you shopping?" Blond Boy asked.

"Nah, we're just looking," Laura said. "We poor and just eating red whips." Laura could have died after she had uttered the last piece of information—*We poor and just eating red whips!* Like how wrong and lame was that?

"What's your names?" Coldplay asked. He stood with his feet pointing in opposite directions, as if one foot wanted to go one way, the other somewhere else.

Laura turned cautiously to Jasmine, who gave her the look, Go ahead, tell 'em. She answered slowly, "She's Alexis and I'm Miley."

"Like Miley Cyrus," Blond Boy said, drumming his hands against his chest. "That's cool."

Laura laughed, but not too widely because she sensed a morsel of red whip between her front teeth, or was it in her eyeteeth? The boys were okay in the looks department and maybe would even be cute once their braces were removed and that volcano-like pimple on Coldplay disappeared. Also it would matter a lot to Laura that his feet pointed straight, not so widely splayed. He looked so ducky.

"Where do you go to school, Alexis?" Blond Boy asked.

Laura could tell that Blond Boy was the dominant guy here. Coldplay had the T-shirt, but the tall Blond Boy was more confident and had a clear complexion and a better posture. Laura assessed her friendship with Jasmine and in a flash calculated that Jasmine was the girl more out front, more boastful, just plain in your face at times.

"Wait a minute!" blurted Jasmine. "Boys first! What's your names?"

"No, the rule is, girls first," Coldplay argued, pointing a finger at Jasmine.

"No sir," chirped Laura.

The two boys looked at each other, their smiles widening.

"I'm Kevin," Coldplay announced. He hooked a thumb at Blond Boy and said, "He's Joe."

"No way!" Laura and Jasmine screamed in near perfect unison.

"You mean like Kevin and Joe from the Jonas Brothers?" Jasmine asked. "Like they're for real."

The two boys folded their lanky arms across their chests. Their heads went like bobble heads. They strummed invisible guitars once and then let their arms hang at their sides.

"Yeah, that's us," said the boy who said he was Joe.

The girls screamed and covered their faces with their hands. They did a stomp and laughed—this was too exciting! Boys with names like the Jonas Brothers! Were they lucky, or what?

"You, like, lie," Jasmine said when her hands came down.

"Shut up," Laura said in a strained but quiet voice, her head lowered but looking out of the corner of her eye at Jasmine, her best friend but what a mouth! Plus, her heart was beginning to thump with a fresh cargo of feelings. She was beginning to like Kevin, who, she decided, was hers. Sure, he was tall for her, also blond, when she was really crazy for dark-haired guys. But what was the big deal? Jasmine, Laura figured, could have Joe. He was short and more her size, and a joker, just like Jasmine.

"Do you like their music?" Laura asked.

"Nah," Coldplay Joe said, almost with a sneer. "It's for girls."

"Girls!" roared Jasmine. "For girls?"

"You know what we mean," Blond Boy Kevin said. "They're like for junior high."

Laura swallowed. She asked, "What grade are you in?"

"Eighth," Joe answered. He scratched his head. "I

know what you're going to say. You're going to say that if we're in middle school, we should dig the Jonas Brothers. But it's not like that. I'm into Spew Face."

"Spew Face?" Jasmine asked with a grimace. "Like barf?"

"Like indie, like not on the radio," Coldplay Joe explained. "You know what I mean? They're so good no one's heard of 'em."

Laura and Jasmine crossed their arms. No one was going to bash the Jonas Brothers. They were too cute to be put down.

"It's like when you're in middle school you got to like things a little older," Blond Boy Kevin explained. "Like we're already thinking about college and that's like, wow, you know, way in the future. I'll probably start at City."

Whatever, Laura thought. It was all too confusing. She asked, "Are your names really Kevin and Joe?"

"Yeah, I don't lie too much," answered Blond Boy Kevin. "Huh, Joe?"

"Right on," Joe answered. "Been Joe all my life, except Grandma Rachel calls me Joseph because she's Catholic, and sometimes Mom calls me Messy."

"More like Goofy," Blond Boy Kevin retorted as he stepped away in anticipation of his friend hitting or pushing him.

"Not even," Coldplay Joe said coolly.

The two pairs began to stroll down the mall, the moment awkward since none of them was extending the conversation. That is, until Jasmine spoke up at the sighting of a HELP WANTED sign in the window at Kids Footlocker.

"That would be an okay job, huh?" Jasmine said brightly.

Laura was glad that Jasmine opened her mouth. Usually she could never tell what string of words, some bad, some good, would roll from her mouth. How many times had Jasmine embarrassed her?

"Yeah," Coldplay Joe said. "I could use a new pair. I could dig some pants, too!" He slapped his thighs and said, "These things are ratty."

"How much do you think they pay?" Laura asked.

"Minimum," Coldplay Joe answered. "But you can steal."

Blond Boy Kevin and Coldplay Joe fist-bumped. They chimed, "Right on!"

When Jasmine said that they were bad, they had to nod their heads—they were grinning at being called bad. They liked that.

They walked in silence past three storefronts before Blond Boy Kevin asked, "Miley, where do you live?"

For a second Laura didn't know whom he was talking to. She was eyeing a little girl in a stroller making the best of the ice cream running down her pudgy arm. Her head was lowered as if she were slurping from a drinking fountain.

"Miley," Blond Boy Kevin called, this time louder.

"Oh, I'm sorry." She brought her stare from the girl

to Blond Boy Kevin. "We live pretty close," she answered vaguely. "We came with our moms."

"Don't lie," Jasmine said, her hand on her cell, which was pink like Laura's, pink like a lot of girls'. She made a face at her cell: nothing.

"What do you mean...lie?" Laura was desperate to spit out to Jasmine that they *should* lie, as they didn't know these boys. Sure, the one she liked, Blond Boy Kevin, was growing from okay to maybe cute. In a few minutes, by the time they reached the American Eagle store at the end of the mall, she might consider him super cute. She was holding out judgment until they circled back and stopped in front of JCPenney. At that point she would decide whether to elevate him to super, super cute and punch his number into her cell.

"She's lying. We came by ourselves." Jasmine explained that she lived only two blocks away on Browning and that they roamed the mall at least once a day, more if they heard rumors of free stuff being given away. She told them that they were almost first in line last week when the Fresno Giants gave away plastic balls and bats.

Laura felt her face redden. Caught lying (or, really, protecting themselves from these trolling boys), she didn't know what to say. She was hurt.

"Are you really in eighth grade?" Coldplay Joe asked.

"Seventh," Laura answered honestly. "We go to Scandinavian."

"Sure you are," Coldplay Joe said. "You're like prob ably sixth-graders."

Jasmine, feigning shock, slapped his arm and said, "You guys are awful."

Laura had had enough of this banter, and enough of them, especially Jasmine, her best friend, maybe her only real friend. But she didn't let on how she felt. She went solo to look in a window of Tommy Hilfiger. The others didn't follow her lead, as she had expected, as she had hoped, as was only right. No, she eyed their reflections in the window as they kept walking, a trio where just seconds ago they were tidy pairs. This made Laura mad at Blond Boy Kevin, who a moment before had been moving into the realm of super, super cute. Why didn't he say something like "It's okay, we don't have to know where you live"? She had to wonder whether *they* were lying about their Jonas Brothers names. She fumed. She thought, If he was my boyfriend, he'd be in big trouble.

But he couldn't be her boyfriend, certainly not after the smooth manner in which he took Jasmine's arm and Jasmine, gazing up at him with a smile, bumped her hip against his. The scandal! Laura found herself swallowing a lump of sadness. Her best friend! Was she a . . . tramp?

"Oh, Jasmine," Laura moaned. "You're such a brat." She was mad at Jasmine for disappointing her. She looked down at her feet, which were pointed straight, not like duck-feet Coldplay Joe. Her toenails were painted bright red, sin red according to the label, and where did it come from, this sudden thought of the baby song "This little piggy went to market, and this little piggy…"? This made her sad, the little rhyme. She remembered her unicorns and horses on her bed. She remembered that she was supposed to be Miley Cryus, but didn't want to be her anymore, or anyone else—just herself, even with all the sad stuff inside her heart and the tears building up in her eyes. She wished that she could hug her favorite pony— that would make her feel good, or at least better.

A few of the stores were rolling down their security gates. A light fluttered, then went dead, at Euphoria. The piped music coming from the speakers stopped. The old men on the bench were gone, but the newspapers remained in disarray. Sunday was over, and Monday would be a day when she would have to decide which new celebrity to become. Jasmine would force her, of this much Laura was sure. Jasmine was just that way, loud and determined to be a celebrity.

But she was tired of that game, and tired of the mall. She didn't have money for anything except a soda and chips. Anyhow, it was all fake.

Blond Boy Kevin turned and, walking backward, waved a hand for her to catch up. There was a smile on his face, then a goofy look when one his sandals came off. He pretended to trip and fall, but it was a bad act.

Laura touched her eyes. No, she wasn't crying, but she wasn't feeling very good, either. She knew that Jasmine was just playing with Blond Boy Kevin when she bumped his hip. That's the way she was, such a tease, not that other word—*tramp.* For all Laura knew Jasmine could be telling the boys that they weren't really Miley and Alexis, but girls with regular names.

"Okay, I'm coming," she said under her breath. *Okay?* She had to wonder what she meant by that. *Okay?* What was okay?

She didn't have time to think about this question. The boys were now walking backward and playing heavy-metal air guitars, and Jasmine, wild Jasmine, was playing a set of invisible drums. They were having fun, or looking like they were having fun. Laura felt that she shouldn't ruin the moment, and hurried over, her hands out and fingers moving across the keys of an organ in a sad melody only she could hear.

It's Not Nice to Stare

As Ashlee boarded the train to New Haven, she felt her bra strap fall onto her bare arm. A middle-aged man dressed in a suit with his necktie undone immediately looked up. She thought, I'm young enough to be his daughter. No, young enough to be his granddaughter. Sick!

She let the strap lie on her arm, toned and tan, and when she lifted her eyes, the lids painted in the lightest blue, another man turned his attention back to the *Times*, reading about war, murders, a dinosaur skeleton in China, and whatever. What did those old men do all day? Whatever it was must be boring.

The train left New Rochelle at 5:47, and now, at 6:14, rocked through Stamford, picking up passengers—office workers, street vendors, loud teenagers, and college students from UConn. There are so many people in the world, she reflected. She wondered whether they had feelings like her own. Was it possible? Did they have the same kinds of emotions as when she fell in love? That happened maybe once a month. Was it that way for everyone? She loved clothes and how they accentuated her figure. She liked music, but her kind of music. She was lost in her thoughts when she noticed a man staring at her.

You wish, she thought. But what did *she* wish? Oh, whatever.

After a while she fitted the bra strap back onto her shoulder. A couple of middle-aged men glanced at her, then went back to magazines and newspapers they were reading—or pretending to be reading. She raised her arms to stretch, showing a little of her midriff.

The men looked.

She was tempted to give them a haughty look, as if to say, It's not nice to stare. But she just pulled her tank top back down and crossed her legs, which were long and lean. She sighed. Most of her friends didn't like their legs, but hers were just fine—as good as any of the models in *Seventeen*. She had the magazine open and had been reading about Linda's problem with Jason, who was seeing the next big star, Melanie, who was the reported daughter of the English rocker Day Ray, who was in rehab but would soon get out. It was all too confusing—who was related to whom. The only thing that could be confirmed was that she had nice skin. Certainly the nicest skin of anyone in her part of the train, which was dirty, though not so dirty that she couldn't sit down, cross her legs, and permit these old men to gawk. Poor old men, she thought. They have nowhere to go but home.

She opened up her compact, and as she was applying lipstick she saw the reflection of an older woman wearing a baseball cap. The woman was looking at her. She's jealous, no doubt, because I have it and she doesn't, never did, and never will. She snapped her compact closed, turned, and almost said angrily, It's not nice to stare.

She spotted a man studying her reflection in the window. He thinks he's so cool, she thought. I know what you're doing! She figured that he might be thirty-eight or something, married but wishing he was sitting next to her. Dream on!

Out of kindness Ashlee dismissed him. She couldn't blame him. But she did wrinkle her nose at the fat girl ambling down the aisle. Dang, what ugly shoes, Ashlee thought with a sneer. I would rather go barefoot than wear those shoes, or the Austin Powers T-shirt. It's probably her brother's.

"You want to buy a candy?" the girl asked.

"What?" Ashlee asked. She noticed stains on the edge of her Austin Powers T-shirt.

"It's for the school," the girl mumbled. The girl had a candy unwrapped, and a big chunk was gone. "It's for cheerleading."

"No," Ashlee answered. Like get out of here, she thought. Like what kind of cheerleaders you got?

The train stopped and picked up new passengers.

Some were big, some were small. Only one boy looked cute, and the girl he was with was just okay. The conductor reported that the train would be delayed. She was hoping to get to Hannah's house by seven.

Ashlee sighed under her breath and fitted her iPod into her ears. She smiled, but not much, as she began to groove to her music. The song was about a girl whose boyfriend doesn't feel that much in love. Yeah, the boyfriend likes me, the singer sings, but he could like me more. Oh, like it's hard.

At that Ashlee began to wonder if there were different levels of love. She remembered liking Bryan but never loving him, and liking Michael but not as much as Bryan. Liking, she realized, was just below love. But was there another experience between liking and loving? She closed her eyes and pictured the singer singing about her boyfriend. Ashlee figured that the boyfriend was probably not a current boyfriend of the singer—no, she probably had moved on, and what the heck, we live and learn.

She then saw a boy her age staring at her. His eyes dropped to the ground and he bent over to pick up a piece of paper from the grimy floor. Like yuck, she grimaced in her mind. She opened her magazine and slapped its page. They won't leave me alone, she thought. They were always looking—boys with pimples and men who were old, older than the delayed train they were sitting on!

When the train lurched, Ashlee woke with a start. For a second she didn't know where she was. She sat up, removing her iPod from her ears. She looked down at her tank top: yes, her little puppy breasts were cute. The poor bald guy in front of her and the poor Hispanic guy behind her. If only people took care of their health and didn't stuff themselves with garbage, they would be more like her...but not exactly like her. She was unique. At least, she thought, that's what Ryan had said. But that was last year.

Then a family of three came swaying down the aisle. The lumpy kids were eating pretzels, chomping away with their mouths open! How rude. When the mother pointed to the seats across from her, she was forced to move her backpack. They sat down, taking all the room. One of the kids bit down on his pretzel as he struggled to pull something from his pocket. It was a packet of mustard, which he tore open with his teeth.

"Give me some," the mother said.

Gross, Ashlee almost said. By the time they're my age, they'll be big as houses! She got up, moved down the aisle—the men were ogling her, she just knew—and sat across from a man in sunglasses.

As she got comfortable, she began to wonder whether he was staring at her from behind his shades. She blocked him from her mind. She plugged her iPod into her ears again and revisited the song of the girl whose boyfriend didn't love her as much as she loved him. She could feel that, the way you could have a boyfriend but not love him all the way because you knew someone better was going to come along eventually. So you saved yourself, she guessed. You didn't give it all away, otherwise you wouldn't have much left when the right one came along.

But she couldn't really get back into the song. That family with pretzels ruined it for her! That ugly boy tearing the mustard with his teeth!

She hoped to be in a better mood when she got to Hannah's house. Hannah's father was like those business guys in suits, but he was nice. He gave her things, like boxes of expensive candies shaped like baby animals. Plus their family had a pool and a lawn where they could put lounge chairs. There were mosquitoes last time, she recalled. But what was perfect? She thought of her legs and her shoulders....

The train suddenly rocked, and Ashlee let out a small scream. Again she had a moment of feeling lost, out of it. Where was she? She pulled her iPod from her ears, looked about sleepily, and stared at the man in sunglasses.

Her mother had snapped once (or was it more than once?) that she was completely self-centered. But Ashlee knew that was untrue. She had only to recall when she gave up her lunch money for a boy who had gotten really hurt in a car accident, and didn't she at least a couple of times give up her seat for old people? At that moment she was feeling sort of sad for the man in sunglasses because his socks didn't match. Poor guy, she brooded.

He probably has only a handful of socks, she figured, and today was one of the days when he had to wear one brown one and one black one.

But he's staring, she thought. He's just totally ogling me. How rude.

But she didn't have time to dwell on this stranger, as the train was pulling into New Haven. Hannah's father would be waiting, and for a second she thought he was sort of okay cute...for someone so old. Once, when he told her he was in his thirties, she recalled he had inflated his chest slightly. Sad, really, but that's what he gets for not working out when he was young.

When she stood up and wiggled her skirt down—it was tight—two men dropped their newspapers to look. She scowled openly at them and really lost it when the man in sunglasses kept staring.

"What are you, blind?" she asked in her anger. "It's not nice to stare!"

The man in sunglasses scratched his nose.

"You're staring!"

Then she saw a cane, the kind that collapses, on the seat next to him. The end had a red band. He *was* blind, and for a moment she hoped that he might be deaf, too. She was embarrassed by her outburst, and wished that she could recant her barrage of words.

The man in sunglasses had his hands laced together, as if in prayer.

"Oh, I'm sorry," she squeaked. She shrugged her

backpack onto her shoulder, which was still tan and lovely. She looked down at her pedicured toes: red as valentines. She hoped that Hannah's father had a box of candies for her.

As she walked down the aisle, two men eyed her hips and her bottom! She turned and almost snapped, Dirty old men! She saw the blind man, whose face was turned toward the window. How sad, she reflected. The poor guy can't see what they see. He never will. I'll be gone and he won't ever know what I look like.

Whose Bedroom Is This?

My bedroom is small as a jail cell. From the center I can take three marching steps this way and touch the windowsill. I can walk four baby steps and touch the door, which opens out instead of in. If I jump I almost touch the ceiling. If I inhale I snatch all the air. A friend once asked, "Is this your closet?" I said, "No, this is my bedroom. Don't you see?" On the wall hang posters of the Jonas Brothers—so cute, all of them, and they can sing!

My bedroom is where my parents store our food and stuff. Let me take inventory: We have three cases of spaghetti wrapped in plastic, nineteen bottles of Gatorade like bowling pins on a shelf, piles of shirts and pants in the ironing basket, and oodles of ramen noodles in noisy cellophane packages. There are four sacks each of rice and pinto beans, laundry soap I could pour on the floor like snow, enough rolls of paper towels to blot out the Gulf of Mexico, and canned soups stacked like the pyramids of Egypt. And powdered milk! I shouldn't say this, but I deplore the taste—*deplore* is the word I learned and used when Mama said I should be grateful for powdered milk. She said, "Think of all the kitty cats who would love that powdered milk!"

What's with this bicycle with no wheels or handlebars? The ice chest and small refrigerator? The boxing gloves big as pillows? What's with this fishing pole? The car stereo that *Papi* intends to sell on eBay? Right now he's slowly tapping his fingers on the arm of his recliner, which, if we could get it down the steps, we would gladly sell and replace with a love seat. His eyes are lit with dollar signs as he, a merchant at heart, has big plans in import/export. He sips his tea, swallows, and reflects on the issue of getting rich. He needs my bedroom to store stuff, for we survive in a one-bedroom apartment overlooking a gray-blue lake. Okay, not a lake but a pond. Well, not even that. It's just a puddle from the two-day rain.

I'm not making this up! My bedroom is more ware house than a place to lay my head on a pillow and listen to my music—Jonas Brothers, I love you! My bedroom is a sort of a Mexican Costco. *¡Los discos!* His pirated Tigres del Norte, Vicente Fernandez, and Luis Miguel! The Spanish-language instructional videos on plumbing and tiling kitchens! Serapes! Piggy-faced piñatas! *¡Dulces mexicanas!* Wreaths of dried chiles. *La Virgen de Guadalupe* votive candles all in a row. *¡Máscaras!* You know, the kind wrestlers wear to scare the crowd and hide their tears when they're thrown from one end of the ring to the other. And let me tell you, we have a dozen used *quinceañera* gowns. If you need a gown the colors of the Guatemalan flag, we've got three. One has a rip down the side, but with needle, thread, and a song on your lips, it's good as new.

My parents sleep in the living room. We're poor but not poor, and my *papi* says it's only a matter of time. His tongue is black from licking the lead of a pencil and adding up the would-be dollars. He doesn't rise before dawn with a face of iron-colored stubble needing a shave. No, he rises after I leave for school, me his precious daughter with a great load of books in my backpack. Is he lazy? No. He argues he needs his sleep and the territory of dreams. It's through dreams, he says, that he'll come up with a scheme. But please don't let it be the lotion he made at the kitchen sink, that yellowish goo that was supposed to soften the roughest skin. He used me as the tester. Oh, God, I smelled like eggs for two days!

Again I make my case. Our apartment is small and getting smaller now that Dad has put on weight. He's fat around the middle. If we could only squeeze him like toothpaste! And Mom? She's so skinny she can hide behind a broom. And she's often scooting through life with a broom, the crazy lady with curlers piled high on her head. How embarrassing! She's always out on the front steps sweeping, waving at gangsters in their lowered cars, and chewing the neighbors' ears off. For a mom who hardly leaves the apartment, she has a lot to report.

When my parents need something late at night, they'll enter my bedroom quiet as mice. That's what I thought the first time. Then I enlarged my fear and thought they might be slick rats with whiskers like wire. But it was just my parents, who are neither mice nor rats. Only last night Mama tiptoed into my bedroom, stubbed her toe against an old computer, hopped, and cried out, "¡Ay, dios mío!" So why did she wake me? For a bag of popcorn to enjoy with a movie. She poured those baby kernels into a pot that rattled and shook over the back burner's flowery flame.

I don't dare open the closet. Cans of food would tumble out—menudo, fruit cocktail, green beans, diced tomatoes, and chipotle sauce brown as my scheming dad. Then there is the vacuum cleaner that resembles an octopus, it has so many tentacles. And what about my *papi*'s Mexican army jacket? Its pockets are filled with sand, his reminder of the place he came from. Why he keeps the army jacket, I don't know. He can't fit into it now that his stomach is round as a globe.

One day my dad brought in a cardboard box that said on the side: CANTALOUPES. But it wasn't filled with melons but with little chicks.

"Why in here?" I asked, backing away, frightened.

"Business, *mi'ja*," he answered with a guilty smile. "Just for a while."

Just for a while! The chicks stayed a week, poor things in their own jail cell! Now you hear them crowing down the street in the early hours. What is next? A calf in my bedroom door—or a devil-eyed goat chewing my bedspread?

Mom made me curtains. She fogged the window with her breath and cleaned it with an old sock. She painted one wall yellow and the other blue—this is all the paint she could find among the clutter. She taught me how to iron. "Isn't this fun?" she sang as she burned the back of a white shirt. "Yeah, Mom—lots," I answered. "Let me burn the front."

This is my family. I can't get away for even a day. In fall *Papi* arrived with a suitcase of hairstyling gear—clippers, combs, scissors, and a small brush to sweep away the mess he would create. In winter he carried in sacks of tulip bulbs—he announced that he was going to go door-to-door spreading beauty, provided, of course, you had a dollar for each Dutch bulb. In spring he announced a second round of chicks. In summer he lugged in watermelons, now in the agricultural import business. He hopped onto a bicycle and rode crookedly down the street, shouting, "*¡Sandías! ¡Sandías deliciosas!*"

I know that parents have to make a living, but did *Papi* have to wear a sombrero? Or did he have to go door-to-door peddling those Dutch tulip bulbs? And that weekend when he decided that his purpose in life was to sharpen knives! Yes, that was another scheme. Hat in hand, his brown face wrinkled like an old wallet, he climbed steps and knocked on doors. "Señor," he would begin, "Señora, señorita. Life is really no more than a beautifully sliced tomato."

This curious life is mine, the thirteen-year-old from Mexico—or born in Mexico but raised here in Cicero for exactly nine years and four months, plus some weeks I suppose. You can call me Mexican, or you can call me Hispanic. You can also call me sort of funny and sort of sad. After all, my bedroom is small as a prison cell. I have penciled the days on a wall: a hundred and thirty-five days since we moved to this apartment where every few minutes you can hear the sound of toilets flushing through the walls. When are we going to move to a house with a big lawn like the kind you see in movies? "Oh, Jonas Brothers," I have wept into my pillow, "please come and save me. Drive me away in one of your limos—*por favor*." I'm only five feet tall, but I'm their biggest fan.

Now winter has arrived with a heck of a storm. The house groans, the lights flicker, and the wind whistles a chilly tune through the rattling window. The trees shake their arthritic limbs and the poor pigeons, the color of old trench coats, huddle under the eaves. The rain, I see, is flooding the street. Plastic water bottles float like buoys. Wet laundry—T-shirts and *chones* from clotheslines— is flying like kites. Lightning flashes over one house and reminds me of having my passport picture taken—flash-flash, and red in my eyes!

There is a bump against my bedroom door. Who else could it be but my father?

"*¿Qué es esto, Papi?*" I ask as he enters, pulling something. "What is that?"

Red-faced, *Papi* wrestles whatever it is in his arms into my bedroom. He lets the thing fall from his arms. Breathing hard, he wipes his face with his sleeve and answers in Spanish, "A boat."

"*Un bateau?*" I repeat in French, the third language I'm going to conquer so in time I can move to France when I'm all grown. Then I say in Spanish in my troubled heart, *¿Por qué no?* Why not? You could never guess what *Papi* will bring home next and haul into my bedroom, a warehouse for every one of his crazy dreams.

"Such a reasonable girl," my father says with pride. He corrects himself, saying that the object on the floor is an inflatable boat. He says, "You can never tell when we might need one."

"*Ay, dios mío,*" I whisper, and search the lines on my palms for my fate.

Papi snatches a bottle of Gatorade from the shelf, his reward for finding such a valuable object in the Dumpster. He closes the door behind him and I hear him in the kitchen. Soon popcorn will be firing like bullets because he'll have forgotten the lid.

But it makes sense—*Papi*, a ranchero still wet behind the ears, sees value in everything. What looks like junk to a rich person is this poor man's riches. And he's thinking of me, his only daughter, who in two years' time will have her choice of any of the *quinceañera* gowns displayed on the wall.

I sit on the edge of my bed. Why read a story or a comic book when you can live in this one-bedroom apartment? Why worry about food? I can reach over to snatch any box of cereal. Or I could pull the tab of a tuna can and eat it with a plastic fork. Maybe the rain will rise and *Papi* will come into the bedroom yelling, "*¡Apúrate!* Hurry up, child!"

That would be great! I could leave behind this crowded bedroom of mine. *Papi* will pump up the inflatable boat (we have two pumps somewhere in the closet), stock it with provisions, and push our rubber ark out of the second-story window, where the risen tide of rainwater will be lapping. How funny! I would never think of jumping out of my bedroom window, but swimming from it? It is possible. The sky is raining big fat cats and dogs. The streets are lakes now, and will soon become a sea.

I can see it now. *Papi* will be rowing with all his might, then stop, mouth open and his thinning hair parted by the pelting rain, and shout, "I forgot the can opener."

By then our apartment will be underwater, but *Papi*, such a wise man, will think of something. Paddling over the small waves, our merchant at heart will be looking about, crowing, "This water, this rainwater. So pure. I think we could sell it." Ever a schemer, he will reach for a plastic bottle bobbing in this lake and fill up the first of so many.

Two Girls, Best Friends, and a Frog

"Choose." That's what Rebecca, a girl from across the street, had once said as she held out two tiny fists. When Freddie pointed to the right fist, she turned it over and opened her hand up like a flower. At the center of her sticky palm lay an unwrapped jawbreaker. Once again Freddie had guessed right! He popped that third jaw-breaker into his bulging cheeks.

He was six years old, and Rebecca only five years old, but her front baby teeth were already gone. Under a plum tree in the front yard they played this game, and lucky Freddy, he got them all—the jawbreakers and the starry jacks, plus the little rubber ball that went with the jacks. He also nabbed a tiny magnifying glass that he used to burn a dry leaf. He remembered the leaf smoking and a fringe of fire eating a hole in the center.

For the first twelve years of his life, Freddie was a great guesser. He was what they called intuitive—he just knew!

Other kids could play soccer, or puff up their cheeks to produce music through a tuba, or do high math, or put together Lego dinosaurs without any pieces left over, but *his* talent was guessing.

He was quick. Just guess! Just choose! His uncle once set a piece of newspaper in front of him. "Can you choose a stock?" his uncle asked. His uncle had driven all the fifty miles from Chowchilla to Fresno when he heard of Freddie's quick mind. His tie was undone, just like his life—undone because the three houses he bought during the real estate boom were now boarded-up foreclosures.

"What's a stock?" Freddie asked. He had been in the kitchen eating powdered donut holes and playing with his Game Boy.

His uncle explained that the symbols were the names of companies worth millions of dollars. Sure enough, with no thought and moving quickly, Freddie chose three stock symbols by the way they looked—PU, BLA, WOW. In the next couple of months his uncle was happy to see that these stocks rose an average of twenty percent.

Freddie's intuition made him a good guesser at a lot of things. He knew what bully boys to stay away from, and which dog was nice and which one would take off your hand with snap.

"What's the capital of Chile?" his teacher asked during a history lesson. "Paris or Santiago?"

"Santiago," Freddie yelled from his chair.

"Which river is longer—the Danube or the Nile?"

Like duh, Freddie thought. "The Nile," he answered.

"Who was the third president of the United States? Polk or Jefferson?"

Easy, Freddie figured. Who had ever heard of Polk? "Jefferson," he offered in a bored voice.

"What came first, the chicken or the egg?" the teacher asked.

For a second he was stumped. He raised a tired arm into the air before he noticed that his teacher was smiling.

"That's a trick question," he answered. He let his arm fall back down onto his desk.

Freddie was good at multiple-choice tests. His sharpened pencil would stab violently at the right answers. He was good at choosing teams at recess, and good at board games like Monopoly. He predicted the president—Mr. Obama. Of course, this was easy because the new president was tall and smart, and the country was in need of someone tall and smart.

On the family front, he picked out a lottery number for his dad. His father won fifty dollars, of which a two-dollar bill went to Freddie. Freddie predicted that the New England Patriots would go to the Super Bowl (he guessed they would get there, not necessarily win) and that the Los Angeles Lakers would win it all in a near sweep. He didn't play golf, and didn't even like that sport because nothing seemed to happen. Still, he often chose Tiger Woods to win, win, win!

I'm just lucky, Freddie mused as he polished a ring he

had found against the front of his T-shirt. He could guess the winners of school elections, the Academy Awards, the Grammys, and even *American Idol*. He knew when he could act stupid in class—he could sense when the teacher would look up, in time to act right. That saved him the time he put two eraser heads in his nose and sneezed them out to make the girls laugh.

Freddie was also plain lucky that he got Mrs. Laird for English and not Mrs. Charles, who was a far harder grader and mean as a snake. He heard that she would strike when you least expected.

For some reason Freddie began to lose his power in eighth grade, a time when he needed it more than ever. He chose the wrong answers on multiple-choice tests and the wrong teams for the playoffs. He lost against his friend Ethan when they played heads-or-tails with dimes.

The stars no longer aligned in his favor. At a critical time, when Freddie was in love with two girls, he couldn't decide which he should choose. He knew that it was not right to flatter himself, but he was aware that he was sort of cute. His hair was nice and bouncy, his teeth straight and white, and his stomach almost flat.

One of the girls was Rebecca, a girl with sticky hands. She had gotten caught stealing candy at Wal-Mart. He heard that she cried and cried in the room where they took you when you stole stuff. But because of her wailing and all the tears, they let her go without pressing charges.

Perhaps they couldn't stand the sight of her open mouth and the half-eaten chocolate lodged there.

Then there was Marta, the only Girl Scout in middle school. Some of the kids made fun of her when she wore her uniform, but she just smiled, sold her cookies once a year, and did special little projects that got her into the school newspaper. She was nice. This is what Freddie liked about her, and that her teeth were white and straight, like his. This is what they had in common.

Freddie had been a Cub Scout himself when he was eight. But his mom never bought him the full uniform, making him feel incomplete with the shirt and cap but without the pants, belt, or kerchief. He made a couple of lanyards, helped with a food drive for the homeless, and was reintroduced to the magnifying glass on a wilderness trip. On that occasion he attempted to start a campfire by burning leaves. But the hungry Scouts blasted him because it was late in the day and the sun seemed strong enough to ignite the leaves without the magnifying glass. Everyone hovered over him, yelling, "Just use matches," "Hurry up," and "On Scout's honor, I'm going to get mad!" Poor Freddie never earned a campfire badge to stitch on his uniform.

Both Rebecca and Marta were pretty. He couldn't decide which girl he liked better, and was so full of uncertainty that he asked Ethan, "Who should I choose?" He fretted because of his lost intuition.

Ethan and he were walking near a ditch hunting for frogs. They were going to bring home a sack of them to sell to Ethan's neighbor. How this neighbor could eat frogs, Freddie couldn't understand. He imagined it would be like eating a rubber glove—strange-colored and chewy.

"I don't know," Ethan answered as he straddled two rocks. "Choose Marta."

"Why?" Freddie asked. He was squatting with his hands on his knees and staring at the murky ditch water.

"Because you're getting a D in Spanish."

Freddie was of Mexican descent but not from Mexico. Marta was, and could speak Spanish that was beyond comprehension to a boy like him. She could sputter *palabras* without having to think about them.

"But don't you think I should choose my girlfriend because I like her?"

Ethan became deaf to his friend's over-grilled conversation. His eyes widened with excitement. "There's one!" He pointed a finger at the water foaming around a board that jutted from the surface.

Hideous-looking frog's eyes lurked in the foam. Ethan stepped from rock to rock in a balancing act that was near miraculous. When Ethan bent over to catch the frog, his shadow—and there was a lot of shadow because he was fat—made it leap away.

"Dang!" Ethan yelled. He stood up, fumed, and moved off the rocks to the safety of the bank.

"What about Rebecca? Don't you think I should choose

her?" Freddie returned to the question that he had hoped to answer by the end of the day.

"Choose her, then," Ethan said with indifference. His eyes were narrowed at the place the frog had blended into the wintry weeds.

"You sound like you don't care," Freddie remarked.

Ethan pulled a handful of sunflower seeds from his pocket and tossed a few into his mouth. He answered, "Yeah, sure, I care," but didn't sound convincing.

Freddie didn't care either when his attention was drawn to what looked like a twenty-dollar bill waving under the surface of the water. Squatting, he plucked it from the water, held it up between wet fingers, and discovered that it was a report card for some kid named Larry Rogers. While the soggy report card was coming apart in his hands, he noted a row of Cs and Ds, plus an F in French. He imagined this doofus Larry Rogers biking to the ditch to drink a soda, burp after each swig (did the frogs answer back? Freddie wondered), and toss the evidence of his stupidity—this report card—into the stagnant water.

If this doofus didn't care, then why should I? Freddie thought. He balled up the report card and flung it away. Again he badgered Ethan with his dilemma: "So should I like Rebecca or Marta?"

"Rebecca. She has big, nasty brothers." He spit out sunflower seeds and returned his meaty paw to his pocket for more.

Freddie pondered this point. Rebecca's brothers were gangsters with tattoos on their pulsating throats. Possibly, if he ever got jammed up by another big kid, he could call on her brothers to help him out. There was plenty of logic behind Ethan's view on the matter.

Now that Freddie had lost his intuition, he understood better why old people lost things. Where are my keys? his grandfather used to ask, grumbling. My glasses! My hearing aid! He sympathized with Grandpa now that his own lucky star and power to guess had vanished.

For the moment he dropped the subject of which girl to choose. He followed Ethan from rock to rock in their frog search. They found one that was too mangled to cook. Ethan picked him up and turned him over and over.

"I feel sorry for him," Ethan said as he set him back in the water. "The guy was hit by a big stick or something. I wonder if his mother ever loved him."

The frog treaded water with his bulging eyes resting on the surface.

"Let's go," Freddie suggested. His shoes were sopping wet and he was getting cold.

In the late afternoon the sun descended and cast chilly shadows that crawled from the ditch and spread. With Ethan on the handlebars, they rode away on Freddie's bike. It was hard going at first. Freddie grunted, strained, and worked up a sweat. His legs burned from exhaustion because Ethan was so heavy. But once the bike got rolling, he returned to his dilemma. So far there were two established points: Marta could help him in Spanish, and Rebecca's brothers could come to his defense if he ever got into a fight.

He managed to find out right away why he should choose the Spanish help. A man on a bicycle sidled up to them and asked them to stop. Freddie recalled from the Boy Scout inventory inside his head that he should do one good deed a day. Do it, he commanded himself. He braked the bike, sending Ethan leaping like a frog off the handlebars and landing harmlessly in the street.

"What, sir?" Freddie asked as he straddled his bike.

The man's face was lined, his eyes red from too much sunlight or beer, and his front teeth capped in gold. The stranger asked something in Spanish, throwing his hands up now and then.

"You know what he's saying?" Freddie asked Ethan.

Ethan shrugged his shoulders.

"WE NO UNDERSTAND," Freddie answered loudly. He shrugged his shoulders and smiled. "*¿Entiendes?*" That was one word that he remembered with certainty, only because his mother always said "*¿Entiendes, Mendez?*" when she meant business. The man pedaled away.

Next, the reason why he should choose Marta with her gangster brothers became clear. The boys were riding smoothly under the autumn sky when a stringy older boy in a white T-shirt ran like a dog next to the bike and grabbed the handlebars. He told them to pull over, or else.

"What do you want?" Ethan asked after he leaped off

the handlebars. He gambled that his puffed chest would make the stringy boy think twice about interfering with their trek home.

"Your life, if you ain't got money. I'm hungry and thirsty."

To Freddie the glue-head didn't seem that big, just stringy. So he swung a leg over his bike, got off, and pushed the bike at Ethan to hold. He balled up his fist, just as his Tae Kwon Do teacher told him to do, and focused on the solar plexus as a place to land a punch.

"If you want our money, then you have to get it," Freddie remarked without considering the consequences. He had in mind Jackie Chan. He wasn't going to be pushed around.

"What did you say, little girl?" The stringy kid had balled up his own hands into impressive hammers, and a fire blazed in his eyes.

Freddie didn't bother to answer. With raised hands, he stood with his legs set apart. He tightened his stomach muscles. He closed his mouth, for now there was no more to say. It was time to fight!

The stringy kid spit between Freddie's legs. It was a glob the color of the ugly frog. As the assailant approached him, Freddie backed up and smartly crumpled to the ground in a defense move, one that he had developed all on his own. He immediately gave it a name: "The Scaredy Kat."

His defensive move didn't stop the stringy kid from

dropping to his knees, slapping Freddie once on the side of the head and rummaging through his pockets. He first searched his front pockets and then rolled him like an enchilada to search his back pockets. Then he turned to Ethan, who, in a fit of common sense, had released the air in his chest so that his stomach now hung like a sack. He froze. The stringy kid shoved his hands into Ethan's pockets, swearing all along as he searched for coins that Ethan smelled like old fish. Ethan didn't bother to explain the frog smell or which pockets held money. Let's get it over with, Ethan wanted to say. But he was starched with fear, and just stood motionless.

After the episode of street piracy, Freddie and Ethan sat on the curb, dejected. Not only had they not caught frogs to bolster their meager resources, but now they were penniless, plus hurt at not defending their honor. What was wrong with them?

"That was embarrassing," Freddie said with his head down. If he had been alone, he would have cried. But Ethan was next to him. Freddie spit at an ant staggering aimlessly in the gutter, and missed badly. He considered smearing the ant with a swipe of his shoe, but was filled with mercy for the little guy with crooked antennae. Why pick on him?

"Yeah, it was. He stole about two dollars." Ethan pinched his stomach fat. He was full of self-loathing. He vowed from that moment to lift weights, lots of them, and eat more fruits and veggies. In a couple of weeks he would make Superman look like a weenie! He would go beyond the six-pack stomach muscles. No, he would have a twelve-pack! He would spank that stringy kid!

Freddie left Ethan making other promises, such as studying mixed martial arts, and rode away in silence. At home he washed the ditch smells off his body, ate six handfuls of barbecue-flavored potato chips, and retreated to his bedroom to repent for his weakness.

Why am I so weak? he asked himself, on the verge of blubbering. Why? Why? Why?

But after ten minutes of self-questioning, he pushed the encounter with the stringy kid to the back of his mind. He put his iPod into action, lay on his bed with his hands behind his head, and bathed his mind in pleasant imagery of Rebecca and Marta. They were cute, and he was sure that they thought he was cute. But of the two, whom did he really like?

By the time his parents called him, Freddie had decided. He leaped out bed and said, "Rebecca, you're the lucky one!"

He made himself laugh. He knew it was conceited to say that, but hey, he was what he was—he had built up his self-portrait from cute to handsome! He text-messaged Ethan, saying, "Rebecca's the one."

The next morning he planned how to entice Rebecca, who he knew had a sweet tooth. He remembered a box of heart-shaped candies in the pantry. They had been there for months, but went uneaten because his mom was on a diet. Freddie figured that his mother wouldn't miss them.

He tucked the box under his coat, and, ninja quiet, sneaked out of the house. He hopped onto his bike and rode to the end of the block, where Rebecca lived. There were cars parked on the lawn, clothes spread out next to them in a yard sale that never ended, and a dog behind a chain-link fence.

"Spike," Freddie greeted him.

Spike wagged his tail and pushed his nose through the fence. Freddie petted the dog's snout with a finger, and felt a glow because every time the dog exhaled white breath emerged from his nostrils like a locomotive.

Freddie's attention was drawn to the front door. He had heard it open, some laughter, and footsteps. Freddie's heart lifted at the sight of a beaming Rebecca coming down the concrete steps. Freddie knew that her happiness could mean only one thing: She also liked him. But seconds later his eyes widened in fear. She had what looked like blood spilling from her wrist, but on second glance he saw that it was a length of red whip candy. He marveled at how his emotions could move from happiness to worry to happiness again. Was this what love was all about? Mixed emotions?

His emotions changed yet again! Behind Rebecca followed a boy—no, not just any boy, but that stringy kid who had jacked Ethan and him over.

Immediately Freddie turned away, but he didn't advance more than five steps before Rebecca shouted, "Hey, Freddie, what are you doing?"

Freddie swallowed as he tried to lubricate his tongue. He turned around slowly and answered meekly, "You mean me?" He pointed a finger at himself.

Rebecca hurried to the chain-link fence. "What you got?" She was breathing hard, and smiling. She sniffed once, then once again. Did she have a cold, or the truly useful ability to smell out candy, such as the box hidden under his jacket?

"Looks like you're buffed," Rebecca said as the stringy guy came up from behind and put an arm around her waist. He had a bored look on his face... or was it stupidity? Freddie wondered.

"You're hiding something, huh?" Rebecca asked. "Either that or you're wearing a bulletproof vest." She reached over the fence and tapped his chest, which produced a hollow sound.

"Who's this fool?" the stringy dude asked.

"Freddie," Rebecca answered. "I told you about him. And don't be like that. We been friends since we were way little." Bending her knees slightly, she made a flat plane of her hand and indicated their height when they first met.

Freddie smiled falsely, offered a solemn "Good-bye," and, head lowered into his coat, began walking away. The moment stung, stung badly. He had never written a poem, but he was going to find out how because only poetry—no, maybe a hit song!—could make him feel better.

But Freddie didn't get far before he felt a weight on his shoulder. He prayed it was nothing but a wayward leaf, but what leaf grasps like an eagle's talon? Freddie turned to peek at the tattooed hand on his shoulder.

"What you got under your coat?" the stringy kid asked.

"Nothing," Freddie managed to answer, though his throat was dry from fear.

"I ought to smack you again, this time on the other side of your head." The stringy kid snaked a hand inside Freddie's coat and, as in an abracadabra magic trick, pulled out the box of heart-shaped candies. The stringy kid smiled and sang, "Oh lookie, a box of candies from pretty boy." His glee faded into a hard stare. He got so close to Freddie that a passerby might have thought they were hugging in friendship. But it wasn't any hug. The stringy kid was telling him that he didn't want Freddie hanging with Rebecca.

"¿Entiendes, Mendez?" the stringy kid whispered.

Freddie nodded, took a step back after the skinny kid poked his chest with a knife-sharp finger, and walked away with his hands in his pockets. It was only ten in the morning according to his cell phone, and already it was a messed-up day. He text-messaged Ethan: "Where are you?" Within seconds he got an answer: "Mayfair Market."

Freddie walked six blocks, his hands now swinging at his sides. He was angry at Rebecca. What was wrong with her! How could she like such a loser? And to think that she and he had been friends since they were in diapers—he had a photo of them together when they were two. Didn't that mean they were destined for each other? Full of pain, he pictured the stringy kid giving her the box of heart-shaped chocolates. Rebecca would jump up and down before hugging him.

A wind stirred the nearly bare trees of November. He wished the wind would blow away the image of Rebecca and her new boyfriend in one big gust. He was mad, he was jealous, he was determined to lift weights and study Tae Kwon Do. In a short time he would confront that stringy kid, beat him with every kick and chop in his arsenal of self-defense, and claim Rebecca as his own.

But the day only got worse when at Mayfair Market he saw Ethan and Marta together. They were standing behind a card table that held a can of pens and pencils. A sign draped on the front said TIOGA SCHOOL FOOD DRIVE. Freddie had a hunch: They were an item, like boyfriend and girlfriend. He swallowed that terrible truth.

"How could you?" he found himself thinking. He felt as if his girlfriend was cheating on him with his best friend. He swallowed again. Life tasted terrible.

Freddie could tell that they were enjoying the moment. Ethan and Marta were laughing, and Marta—the gesture nearly shattered his heart!—had suddenly slipped her arm inside Ethan's. It seemed so natural, her hand on his friend's fat arm. Were they in love? His eyes were ready to rain tears.

"Hey," Ethan called. He waved to Freddie and called in a friendly voice, "Hey, get over here!"

Marta was dressed in her Girl Scout uniform. She had a sash with dozens of badges, and one large one on her cap.

"No, I got to go," Freddie muttered weakly. He raised an arm as if he knew the answer to this situation. Unlike the times when he was in elementary school and could answer simple questions, this one seemed too complicated. He did the only right thing. He hurried away in spite of Ethan's pleading, "Where are you going?"

Two blocks away, Freddie called Ethan on his cell phone.

"What are you doing with Marta?" Freddie asked. "I thought you were my friend."

"What do you mean?" Ethan asked.

Freddie explained himself.

"W-w-well," Ethan began with a stutter. "You said you liked Rebecca. Didn't you? You told me this morning." Freddie argued that Ethan could at least have waited for a day because maybe he was wrong, maybe Rebecca wasn't the right girl.

"But you said," Ethan countered. "You told me." Ethan confessed that he liked Marta, had always liked her. He said that she liked him, too.

Freddie hung up, fearing any kind of elaboration. He fumed. He kicked a plastic cup into the gutter, and thought his heart belonged in the gutter, where the strongest of the strongest ants would carry it away. It should be in a shrine down below where the ants lived, he thought, on the verge of tears.

Dejected, Freddie plodded with heavy steps to the ditch. There he sat on a large rock with his head in his hands, and wondered what had happened. Family and friends said that he had been born under a lucky star. He briefly lifted his eyes skyward and then returned his gaze to the murky ditch water. They said he was a good guesser, was full of intuition, and was good at choosing. If so, why hadn't he had the sense to choose the right girlfriend when he had the chance? Why had he been so slow?

"I don't care," he mumbled. He tossed a small pebble into the water, and was determined that his heart would be just a stone in the future. Yes, a stone without feeling! He touched the corners of his eyes to see if he was crying. He looked at his fingertips. No tears.

Just then the ugly frog that he and Ethan had released leaped from the water onto a rock. The frog gazed sleepily at Freddie for the longest time before it said something in frog language that probably was "Yeah, Freddie, I know how you feel. I once had two girl frogs, but I just couldn't choose."

Freddie and the frog then had a staring contest. When Freddie looked away—he was tired of looking at the ugliest frog in the world—he hitched up his pants. He pitched a rock into the ditch and walked back home, alone.

Altar Boys

With his eyes closed, Little Ray rolled out of bed at 6:45 in the morning and stumbled blindly to the bathroom, where he stood at the sink, still more asleep than awake. He reached for the faucet, gave it a crank, and let the water run warm before he cupped a handful and tossed it at his face. Both eyes sprang open and were remarkably clear, considering that he hadn't gone to bed until after *Saturday Night Live* ended.

It was a Sunday in early March. Little Ray and his friend Jesus were scheduled to put on altar boy skirts and blouses and assist Father Mario, who often looked as if he was asleep at the altar. Father Mario had circles dark as midnight under his eyes, and dried shaving cream around his large, hairy, elephant-like ears. Stiff bristles of hair sprouted from his frighteningly large nose.

"Poor Father Mario," Little Ray had once lamented. "He always gets eight o'clock Mass."

Little Ray dressed in his previous day's clothes, which smelled of grass, oil (he had helped his father locate a leak under their car), and sweat. His socks were stiff from sweat and dirt, but he figured they were good enough to house his feet for just another day. He shrugged into a jacket. Before exiting by way of the kitchen, he grabbed a banana and a trumpet-sized *chicharron*, a fried pork rind that nearly broke his teeth. It was one of his favorite treats—that and pickled pigs feet, which he and his father shared when they watched the Oakland Raiders on television.

The sun rose tiredly over the roofs of the neighborhood. It was the quietest time of day, quieter than night, when every neighbor's television or radio was blaring some sort of noise. Even the dogs behind the chain-link fences were asleep. Pecas, the neighbor's dog, opened his eyes to assess the sound of Little Ray's first crunching bite of *chicharron*, then closed them and went back to sleep.

Little Ray started toward St. John's Catholic Church. There Jesus was waiting in front. At first Little Ray had a crazy notion that his friend was brushing his teeth. Little Ray rubbed his eyes. No, not brushing his teeth, his friend was eating a . . . chicken drumstick?

"Dang, Jesus, what you are eating?" Little Ray asked as he approached the friend he had known since first grade. "Can't you wait until after service?"

Jesus's front teeth were pulling the skin off like a sock. He chewed noisily, swallowed, and cleared his throat. "It's okay. We ain't needed. Father gave me this anyhow." He swung the drumstick like a conductor's baton, and said that it was left over from Sylvia Mendez's *quinceañera* the night before.

"Why?"

"Someone messed up the schedule. Samuel and Juan are doing it. I'm glad." He lowered his teeth back to the drumstick. Within five bites all the meat was gone. Jesus tossed the bone into the trash can and licked his greasy fingers.

"Sylvia had her *quinceañera?*" Little Ray had a crush on Sylvia in fourth and fifth grades. Now that he was in eighth grade, he had warm feelings for her again. "How come she didn't invite us?"

"Because we'd eat everything. Man, I could use a soda." Jesus licked first his left, then his right pinkie for more taste of chicken, and was about to say something when out of the corner of his eye he noticed a boy on a gas-powered scooter weaving crazily.

Little Ray turned to the gnat-like whine of the scooter heading their way. He had always considered owning a scooter to be a rite of passage, that and kissing his first girl. But his father squashed that dream like an aluminum soda can. "You'll get killed," he would argue, "and then what are you doing do, huh? *Nada.* You'll be in the grave with worms up your nose!"

But the approaching scooter made his heart thump with excitement. It bumped up onto the sidewalk, scattering a few of the parishioners. Little Ray noted that the kid was about his age. His eyes were yellowish with fear, and he had good reason. Seconds later two other kids, bigger ones puffed up in large jackets, rounded the corner on bikes.

They're going to drag him down, Little Ray thought. He recalled a *National Geographic* episode of a high-speed leopard pursuing a gazelle. This was almost the same thing, except that where the animals were graceful and pretty, these boys were just plain ugly.

The kid on the scooter sailed off the sidewalk and hit the street awkwardly, the front wheel turning sideways on impact. Hands out, the kid went flying over the handlebars as if diving into a pool. Instead of hitting water, this victim of hard knocks hit asphalt. He rolled and, wincing from pain, scurried to his feet. He ran away, his arms tucked to his sides.

The two boys on bikes pursued him, their long legs pumping the pedals hard.

"Wow," Jesus crowed.

Little Ray and Jesus hurried over to the scooter, whose engine was still running. A plume of blue smoke coughed from its tiny exhaust pipe.

"Let's go," Jesus said.

"What?" Little Ray asked breathlessly. "That's stealing."

"Nah, we'll bring it back. We're just going for a ride. Get on, dude!" Jesus picked up the scooter and gunned the engine.

With his heart beating in excitement, Little Ray hopped

on and gripped Jesus's shoulders. Jesus gunned the engine and, as they slowly rode away, Little Ray thought, We're not stealing, not really. The scooter was just abandoned in the road. Still, he felt like a criminal escaping the law. Then his eyes locked momentarily on the faces of his aunt and uncle, members of the early-riser parishioners, who were walking arm in arm. He thought, Ah, man, they're going to tell my parents. His aunt and uncle stopped and looked at their nephew. They appeared confused.

"I'm busted," Little Ray yelled in Jesus's ear.

"What?" his friend asked.

"Nothing," he answered. He thought of his father, who would kill him if he learned from relatives that his son was tooling around on a scooter. Then, for sure, slimy worms would wiggle up his nose, for he would be major dead.

But their Sunday escapade didn't advance more than a hundred yards before Little Ray tugged Jesus's sleeve. He yelled, "Look!"

A second scooter, the engine dead, lay in the street.

Jesus circled back. Little Ray jumped off, picking up the scooter and bringing it to life. He gunned the engine, hopped on, and trailed Jesus, who was already managing his scooter expertly with only one hand on the handlebars. His free hand was scratching his armpit.

Two blocks later they slowed to a stop. Little Ray's eyes were dry from the wind. The hair on his head stood up like weeds. His nose was red as Santa's.

"Man, I think we like stole them," Little Ray remarked as he pounded the handlebars with his fists, "and on Sunday."

"They were already stolen," Jesus countered. He cut the engine and bent down to check the level of gas in the tank. The gasoline swished in its plastic tank, which was smaller than a water bottle.

"You think we can keep them?" Little Ray asked.

"Who's big enough to take them from us?" Jesus struck the air with a couple of jabs. "I got a yellow belt in Tae Kwon Do." He raised his leg and threw out a wobbly kick.

But the two boys suddenly became slack-jawed as they sighted two boys in hooded sweatshirts approaching from down the street. Their hands were deep in their pockets.

"Get over here, fat boy," one ordered.

Little Ray thought the thug was referring to Jesus, who was a little heavier than he. But he breathed in and out and saw his stomach rise mountainously, and considered the possibility that the approaching figure was speaking to *him*.

"Get over here, ugly!" he yelled.

Ah, Little Ray concluded. He *must* be referring to Jesus. Nevertheless he was scared. The thug's front tooth was gold, or was it just yellow? Little Ray couldn't tell, and wasn't about to stick around talking about the best places to get a new set of grills. He beat Jesus by a fraction of a second in lifting his scooter. He thumbed the starter on the handlebars. The two-stroke engine came alive right away, as if it, too, had enough brains to think, Let's bounce.

"Hurry!" Jesus shouted, his attention turned to the other boys, who were straddling their bicycles in the middle of the street. One was yapping on his cell. When the boy flipped the cell closed, Little Ray cussed. "Dang."

Jesus revved his engine.

"Hey, we wanna talk to you!" one of the boys shouted. "Don't move! I mean it, man." He had taken a Tootsie Roll sucker out of his mouth to threaten them. He cussed at them and threatened to deliver a few jabs at their ugly faces.

"Yeah, right," Little Ray muttered to himself. He gunned his scooter and roared away, scattering pigeons in blue exhaust.

They rode two blocks before they dared to look back. With that distance between them, they figured it was safe to stop and catch their breath. They sat on someone's lawn, exhausted. Jesus rubbed his stomach and said, "Man, I'm hungry."

The two boys lay back for a few minutes, then rose to their feet. Little Ray brooded over his behavior. He had taken a scooter that didn't belong to him, and now God was punishing him.

"Should we lose these things?" Little Ray asked, kicking the front tire of the scooter.

"Why?" Jesus said, gripping the handlebars possessively.

"Oh, yeah, that's right, you know Tae Kwon Do."

"I do! I got my yellow belt under my bed."

"It's more like Tae Kwon Run." He made this remark with a smirk, but the smirk widened into a mask of fear when he made out the boys, plus others, at the end of the block. They were like those leopards, and he and Jesus were the gazelles. The posse on bikes was ready to run them down.

"Let's go," Little Ray yelled.

They rode with their faces like hood ornaments on the handlebars. They risked looking back only when Holmes Playground, their hangout, came into view. Coach Ramirez, a bodybuilder with a most impressive six-pack, might be there to protect them.

As it was only 8:35 in the morning, he wasn't there. But waiting for them was an officer of the law, who was certainly no bodybuilder. But he did possess a bark.

"Where did you get those?" the cop asked in a scorching tone.

Little Ray smacked his lips and squeaked, "Get what, sir?"

"The scooters! What do you think I'm talking about?"

Little Ray and Jesus looked at the scooters.

"We found them in the street," Jesus volunteered.

The cop shook his head at the boys. There was no mirth behind the grin that he put on his face.

"Really, sir," Little Ray said, slightly hurt that the cop didn't believe them. "We were at church when—"

"Church!" the cop nearly yelled. "Yeah, and I bet you're altar boys, too."

"Actually, we are, sir," Little Ray said. He considered saying a prayer to demonstrate their religious calling.

"How come you're all dirty, then?" the officer barked.

The two boys looked down at their clothes. True, Little Ray thought, they weren't exactly in their church clothes. Still, he tried to explain.

"You see, we wear altar boy skirts and blouses, and people can't—"

"Shut up, you little fools," the cop scolded. He approached the boys, his bulky shadow sliding between them. "What's this?" he asked, tapping the shield on his chest.

"Your badge," Jesus spoke up with not much punch.

"Right!" He roasted their ears by saying that he had been on the force for twelve years, and recognized liars when he heard them. He tossed the scooters into the trunk of the cruiser and prodded the boys into the back. He slammed the door none too nicely.

"We didn't do anything," Jesus whimpered to Little Ray.

"You got that right," Little Ray agreed.

Jesus then sniffed and made a funny face. "It smells."

"Yeah, it does." Little Ray sniffed, momentarily wondering whether the odor was coming from Jesus or himself. After all, a part of his wardrobe was that pair of funky-smelling socks. He lifted his shoes and checked the soles: *nada*. He figured that the smell lingering in the backseat must have come from the previous occupant, some criminal who hadn't bathed in days.

When the cop got in, the cruiser rocked from his impressive weight. Little Ray thought the cop, a miniature rhino, was definitely out of shape and possibly an embarrassment to the force. If the cop had tried to ride the scooter, he would have flattened the tires and burned out the two-cycle engine. But Little Ray wasn't about to voice his thoughts. He recognized that he and Jesus were in trouble. He only asked: "It smells in here. Can you roll down the window?"

"It smells?" the cop asked, looking over his shoulder. He grinned.

"Yeah," Jesus answered.

"That's because I've been working the night shift and got BO. You got a problem with that?" He chuckled and clicked his seat belt.

Head down, Little Ray and Jesus pouted at the sticky floor.

The radio squawked. There was static and then a tired voice that said, "Domestic on Thomas Street." She gave the address and sighed.

"Car nineteen," the cop radioed. "I'll take it—ten four." He turned the engine over, adjusted his mirror, and got the cruiser moving slowly, as if whatever mayhem occurring on Thomas was not urgent.

Jesus studied Little Ray, whose face was sad as a clown's. His shoulders, usually square, were slumped and his fingers tightly laced, as if in earnest prayer. And was that moisture in his eyes, the start of tears?

"Are you crying?" Little Ray asked.

"Just a little bit," Jesus answered truthfully, and wiped his eyes.

"This is not fair," Little Ray mumbled. His cousin was a lawyer who worked for the poor, and the poor were as numerous as ants on a jam jar left out on a drain board. His cousin often ranted about how the police mistreated the people they were supposed to protect. Little Ray was beginning to warm up to the idea of announcing to the cop that they were citizens—young ones, true—and that they, like anyone else, had rights. He almost blurted Where are you taking us? when the cop, a mind reader, said, "I don't want to hear a peep from you altar boys."

"But we really are," Little Ray risked.

"It's true," Jesus added. "Ask Father Mario. He wouldn't lie."

Little Ray licked his lips and began to recite a prayer to demonstrate beyond a shadow of a doubt that they were altar boys. But his effort at converting the cop came to a halt.

"What did I say?" The cop's bared teeth appeared in the rearview mirror, which shut Little Ray up. He pushed the image of his ranting cousin to the back of his mind.

The ride was as slow as a slowly moving cloud, but they eventually turned down Thomas Street, where they were greeted by a dog spraying the fender of a parked car.

Little Ray would have laughed, but he wasn't in the

mood. There was nothing funny from where they were sitting.

The cruiser slowed to a stop in front of a duplex. On the brownish lawn there was a scattering of clothes, toys, furniture, bicycles—a yard sale of stuff that no one really needed. The dog that had just relieved himself was now poking his nose among the items. He lifted his leg against a tricycle and spurted.

The cop said, "I'll be right back." He got out, rocking the car. He holstered his nightstick, pulled up his pants, and crossed the street to the address of the domestic disturbance.

"Did you see the dog?" Little Ray asked. "He did it on the trike!"

"Yeah, I saw him," Jesus answered. "He's just a dog. He doesn't know better." This comment forced Little Ray to reflect. He did know better. He should have known that gaffling the scooters was wrong, wrong, wrong. He was brooding when from across the street he spotted a girl bending over and picking up the Sunday newspaper. She was in her bathrobe and wearing furry pink slippers.

"Isn't that Sylvia?" Little Ray asked.

"Sylvia Mendez?" Jesus asked, squinting. "Oh, yeah, it is." He knocked on the window to get her attention. The boys rocked in their seats, swaying the cruiser.

Sylvia was *guera*, light-skinned, and had green eyes. But she was all Mexican and was president of the Spanish

Club. She crossed the street in her robe. She stood a few yards from the cruiser, her hand up as if in salute to shade her brow. "Little Ray?" she asked. "Is that you?"

"Yeah," he roared, his breath fogging to the glass.

"What happened?" she asked nervously.

"It's all a mistake. Me and Jesus—"

"Jesus," she began as she took a step closer to the cruiser, "is that you? Are you in trouble?"

"Not really," Jesus answered. "How was your *quinceañera*?"

"It was nice."

"Father Mario gave me a drumstick from the party," Jesus said. "Did you get a lot of money?"

Little Ray couldn't believe this trivial discussion. The real issue was their confinement in the backseat of a police cruiser. Hadn't they been kidnapped unfairly by the police? What had they really done? They just picked up the scooters that had been abandoned. He said, "Sylvia, try the door."

"Are you crazy?" Jesus asked. "You mean like escape?"

"Yeah, homes, I'm serious. I don't want my parents to find out."

Sylvia yanked open the door, and Little Ray was the first to scoot out on his butt. Jesus followed, remarking, "It smells good out here." He breathed in and out.

"Yeah," Little Ray agreed. "Freedom smells good."

"What did you guys do?" Sylvia's fingers went into her mouth and she began to nibble a fingernail.

"Nothing," Little Ray said. "He just nabbed us. We were just riding these scooters. They're in the trunk."

"Oh," Sylvia chirped. She yawned and said, "I didn't get to sleep until two."

"It was a heck of a party, huh?" Jesus asked Sylvia, who now had her arms wrapped around her chest, suddenly self-conscious about standing in the road in her robe and slippers.

"It was nice," she said. "I think I got a little over three hundred dollars." She wiggled her slippers at them. "My mom got me these."

"Cool." Little Ray whistled. "But we gotta go. We owe you one, Sylvia." Skipping backward, he told her that she had brought justice to the world when she opened the door for them.

"I'll buy you lunch for a week," Little Ray promised.

"You will?" she asked as her face brightened with a smile and her cheeks flushed the color of her pink slippers. "You know I'm a big eater."

He nodded his head, his heart warming up to the idea of Sylvia becoming his girlfriend. He turned, sped away with Jesus at his side, and headed into the alley.

"What should we do?" Jesus asked.

Little Ray, the strategist, had already made plans—they should return to church. There they could help serve donuts for the ten o'clock service or maybe wash Father Mario's car. They would scout the pews for crumpled bulletins and chewing gum wrappers. In short they would play up their humble roles as members of the oldest church in Fresno. If the cop showed up at church, Father Mario would defend them, saying, "Impossible! These are altar boys. They are good kids!" Father Mario would make a sermon of their good deeds and even fit their heads with halos. He would shoo away the cop as if he were a pesky fly.

"Yeah, good idea," Jesus replied. "There's some more chicken in the refrigerator."

"Let's not talk about food," Little Ray said righteously.

"Why not? I like food," Jesus countered. "It keeps me alive."

"Why not?" Little Ray asked, his anger building up a head of steam. "Because we're in deep doo-doo. We're criminals."

"We're not criminals. We're free as the air." He inhaled and exhaled to make his point.

Little Ray, sensing that he wasn't reaching Jesus, poked him in his chest and yelled, "We're in trouble—get it, fool?"

Jesus tottered from the push, waving his arms about and almost falling over.

Such a poor actor, Little Ray smiled to himself, as he had hardly touched him.

Slightly bowed and grimacing, Jesus uttered in pain, "Okay, okay, I'll go. You don't have to get violent." He was midway into his Tae Kwon Do pledge of nonviolence when a police cruiser appeared at the end of the alley.

"Dang," Jesus yelled.

"Aw, man," Little Ray cried.

The menacing cruiser sat idling. Then it began to move toward them, rocking over the potholes. The boys ran.

The last time Little Ray had run away was from Mackenzie Chang, a girl in his class. She had a sprig of mistletoe and was intending to twirl it over his head and plant a wet kiss on him. Now here he was again, running for his life.

"This way," Jesus yelled as he hurdled a pile of grass clippings and leaped onto a garbage can, scooted himself onto a fence, and jumped into a yard.

But before Little Ray could boost himself onto the garbage can, Jesus was leaping *back* over the fence.

"What?" Little Ray asked.

"There's a pit bull there," Jesus explained breathlessly. His eyes, already wide with fear, grew even wider at the sight of the cruiser rolling toward them with chirping squeaks.

Little Ray had watched his share of video games and had learned that sometimes the bad guy—the cop, in this instance—won. But he could at least try to outmaneuver his pursuer. He couldn't be a quitter, not now, not ever. He shuddered at the possibility of his father sentencing him to hard labor. He could see his father pronouncing his verdict: "Boy, you're going to pick, claw, and shovel every flower bed until the end of time."

"Help me," Little Ray pleaded. He began to flip over trash cans, one after another, creating an obstacle course. The cop, swearing up a storm, would have to get out of his cruiser to remove them. They tossed over five garbage cans that spilled their frightful contents, and jammed away.

At the end of the alley they debated going left or right. They chose right and, in the process, returned to the same street where the domestic disturbance had occurred or was occurring or was about to occur or might occur—men with mean faces were acting up all hours of the day.

They leaped under a hedge and, breathing hard as locomotives, flattened their bodies to the ground. Sweat crawled like ants down their foreheads.

"Do you think he'll find us?" Jesus asked.

"Be quiet," Little Ray warned. "And don't move."

They lay quietly until their breathing became normal. Little Ray reflected once again: They should have never taken those scooters. God was watching them and didn't like the havoc they were creating on the streets of Fresno.

Then their ears perked up at the roar of an engine and the peel of tires. The cruiser had turned right, too, and was now slowly making its way up the street. It stopped once, started again and drove a few feet, and stopped another time.

Little Ray had closed his eyes and, behind those lids, pictured himself being yanked to his feet by that burly cop. He saw himself pitched like a sack of garbage into the back of the smelly cruiser. In the next image he was at a police station, where a lady cop was pressing his inked fingertips onto a small card. He was now a registered offender.

But the cruiser pulled away. After a few minutes the boys rose to their feet, slapped leaves, grass and dirt from their clothes and hair, and slowly took a few steps. When Little Ray was twelve, he went out for wrestling and posted almost all losses. And always after these defeats he felt so weak that he could barely walk off the mat. That's how he felt at the moment: weak in the arms and legs.

When they saw the cruiser turning around, the two boys, pants falling off their butts, began to run. The found their second wind. This reservoir of strength became unlocked, and they were soon breaking their own personal records. They returned to the alley, scaled a fence, and fell into a yard where an old lady was hanging up laundry. They offered sincere apologies. They ran along the side of her house and back to the street where they had just been lying facedown underneath a hedge.

"Little Ray," a lilting voice called.

Little Ray, fox-like, raised his face skyward and looked about wildly. Then he saw: Sylvia Mendez was beckoning them. She was now dressed in jeans, hoodie, and sandals.

They hustled over.

"Is he still after you?" Sylvia asked.

The boys nodded.

"Then come inside," Sylvia ordered.

The boys sprinted up onto her porch. They wiped the soles of their shoes, as they were unsure where they had stepped, and entered her house. Sylvia's father sat in a recliner reading the newspaper. He swiveled his head, frowned, and sat up as he took off his reading glasses. The newspaper in his paw seemed to wrinkle from his grip.

"Dad, these are some boys," Sylvia introduced them.

"Some boys," he repeated in a low voice.

Sylvia's father was not a welcoming sort. Little Ray couldn't blame him, either. Their faces were sweaty and their hands were dirty from handling the scooters, jumping over fences, and tossing over smelly garbage cans. Plus, they probably gave off the odor of fear and adolescent sweat.

"Hello, sir." Jesus quickly offered a smile as a sign that they were okay boys.

"Some boys," the father repeated as he rose to a giant stature. His belt buckle that read "Raider Nation" was shiny as a cop's shield. His hands were plumber's wrenches.

Little Ray was convinced that Sylvia's father was going to squeeze the backs of their necks and guide them none too nicely to the front door. Would he blame him? Nah, because they were trespassing on what was, for most, a quiet Sunday morning of *huevos con* weenies, plus stacks of tortillas, *papas*, and maybe *pan dulce.*

But their forced exit never happened, because Sylvia's mother entered the living room clipping on an earring.

She was wearing a white dress and her hair was done up. She stopped, appraised the boys, and smiled.

"Who are these young men?" she asked warmly. Her sweetness disarmed Sylvia's father, who stood there blinking. He sat back down in his recliner, but kept a stern eye on them.

"They're boys from school, Mom," Sylvia explained. "This is Ray and this is Jesus."

The two boys smiled widely.

"We're altar boys," Jesus volunteered. He turned to Little Ray. "Huh, Little Ray?"

"Yes, it's true, Mrs. Mendez, we're altar boys at St. John's."

"Do you need a ride?" Sylvia's mother asked. "I'm going right now."

The boys nodded.

"Let me get my purse," the mother said, disappeared into the kitchen, and returned with cartons of orange juice. "You look thirsty."

The boys accepted her kind gesture. They said good-bye to Mr. Mendez, who was back to reading the sports page, and told Sylvia that they would see her at school. She wouldn't be going to church. She had to clean up after the party, and even said that she was sorry that she hadn't invited them. Her *quinceañera* party had been mostly for family.

The boys jumped into the backseat of the car and, law-abiding citizens from that moment on, buckled their seat belts without being asked. As they neared the church, the boys spotted the guys on bikes. Like vampires, they were still lurking by the church, waiting for those who had gaffled their scooters to return.

Mrs. Mendez parked the car, beeped it locked, and walked between the boys as the three headed toward the church. Little Ray had never felt so free, so happy. He inhaled the sweet-smelling spring air. He spied robins chirping in the trees that were throwing open their blossoms.

They were walking up the steps when Little Ray heard a familiar voice, one he had lived with since the beginning of *his* time.

"Ray," the voice scolded.

The voice belonged to his mother, a devotee of the ten A.M. Spanish-language service.

"Oh, hi, Mom," he tried cheerfully. His face was darkened by her shadow, for she was a large woman. Even her hairdo was big and added inches to her stature. The purse on her arm was like a briefcase, a sign that she was all business. She approached them with one suspicious eye closed. She waited for an explanation, which poured messily from Jesus, who said, "We weren't needed. The schedule was like messed up."

"What?" Little Ray's mother barked. Her hands were now on her hips, a sign she meant business.

"It was messed up," Jesus said incoherently. "Totally whacked! Juan and Samuel got to be altar boys."

But the interrogation by Little Ray's mother was postponed when Laura Mendez introduced herself and said, "They're friends of my Sylvia."

Little Ray's mother released her stare from Little Ray and turned to Mrs. Mendez. "Were these boys any trouble?" she asked.

"Oh, no, they were very nice," Mrs. Mendez said. "They were just in the neighborhood and I gave them a ride."

Little Ray's mother returned her gaze to her son, as if to ask, In the neighborhood? The gaze had some heat to it.

The two women said their good-byes, and Little Ray and Jesus, not forgetting their manners, also said their thank-yous and good-byes.

Little Ray's mother, Little Ray, and Jesus strode up the steps and into the cavernous cathedral pumping out organ music that sounded like a death march. They dipped their fingers into the holy water, an action that worried Little Ray because he imagined that he was polluting the water.

The three found a pew, knelt to offer private prayers, and rose when Father Gabriel, the Spanish-speaking priest, appeared in a white cloud of a robe. Neither Little Ray nor Jesus spoke much Spanish, and they would just have to follow Little Ray's mother's lead.

Little Ray knew that his mother was going to grill them about their sudden appearance at such a Mass. So he prayed, and prayed hard, first in English and then in what little he knew of Spanish.

"Are you in trouble?" his mother asked just before Communion. She had worry lines wiggling across her forehead.

"Nah, Mom, we're okay," Little Ray said.

Then they knelt for prayer, and Little Ray was hoping for a miracle or at least a prayer that would get them through this hour, for his mother had sniffed, soured her face, and said, "Did you step in something?"

Little Ray felt sweat spring into his armpits. He crossed himself and said, "Nah, Mom, we're clean. We ain't done nothing—honest!"

Little Ray's mother shook her head slowly. She knew lying boys when she saw them, and these, in dirty clothes, were stinking of one terrible tale.

"*Ay, dios mío,*" she muttered solemnly at her praying hands. "And to think, O God, that these two are altar boys."

Romancing the Diary

"Today I ate a bowl of cereal for lunch," Monica wrote at the kitchen table in the unlined diary she'd received years ago for Christmas. At that time she considered it a dull gift and, facing the Christmas tree lit with pulsating red lights, formed the word *boring* on her lips. She admonished herself now for ever thinking that such a lovely gift—a diary with an array of flowers on the cover—was boring.

But she had been eight then, a freckled brat. Now, at thirteen and a devourer of novels and poetry, she appreciated her aunt's gift, for she could whisper her deepest secrets into its crisp pages. She was different now. Even the freckles on her nose had disappeared, going wherever freckles go when you suddenly become a teenager. She had grown and grown, and was taller than either of her parents. Her father called her "My precious giraffe." Her mother said: "You're going to change the world."

Monica felt mature beyond her years. True, she had

eaten a bowl of cereal for lunch when she could have had chips, soda, and possibly a candy bar. But she just felt like eating lightly now that she was in love—and wasn't love like a cloud, like a blossom in the wind, like a balloon released to the wild, wild wind? She wrote: "I'm going to see Matt today. I love him so much. He loves me even more. He said he would wait for me at two o'clock."

Monica glanced up at her clock, a plastic cat with its tail wagging left and right as it beat out time. In happiness she turned inwardly to Matt, the boy whom she had liked since she was eleven and used to watch from the height of a play structure in elementary school. He was good at sports and built for play. Back in sixth grade he was cold and rough as wood. One time he snarled at her, all because she suggested that she help him with his homework—her motive, she admitted, was to pull him off the soccer field so that she could have him to herself. It hurt her, that snarling face of his. Had she come on too strong?

Monica figured that sixth-grade boys were just that—boys with not too much upstairs. He just liked to play with other boys. The knees of his jeans were grass-stained, if not torn, and his elbows were often scabbed over from sliding into bases or falling from his skateboard. His dark hair held enough grass and leaves to make a small bird's nest. His neck—yuck!—often had a necklace of dirt.

But they were in eighth grade now. Sometimes Matt still seemed cold and rough, though she thought he liked her. She thought of the word *falling*. "I'm falling," she wrote in her diary. "I'm falling hard, but Matt will catch me because he's strong." She saw herself falling not from a great height, but perhaps from her garage roof. She saw Matt, oh, strong Matt, catching her and burying his face in her hair. She would then kiss him, yes, kiss him for saving her life!

She forced the image to pop like a soap bubble. It was too, too much! Her cheeks had reddened and heat radiated off her ears.

"I'm so silly," she found herself saying. She flipped through her diary and stopped at October 15, which read: "I saw Matt with his stupid friends. He's cute, but his friends aren't, especially Robert. I told Matt that I would help him with his algebra if he liked." She turned to October 9, which read: "I think Matt is sick because he's not at school. There was a speaker who came to school today to talk about traffic safety. Really boring." She noticed as she flipped through the pages that she sometimes used a pink pen, other times a black pen. A couple of times she wrote in pencil. On each page she had drawn a heart.

It was all there, her life story, in this diary. There was the day she got her braces, and the day she found a ten-dollar bill. There was the day she got shot down in a classroom spelling bee—how was she supposed to know how to spell *euphoria*?—and the day it rained so hard that school was cancelled. There were deep emotions, too, like when her mother told her that her mother—Monica's grandmother—had cancer.

Monica got up, the chair scooting noisily on the linoleum floor, and walked the short distance to the sink for a drink of water. She scrutinized the avocado pit lanced with toothpicks on the windowsill. It's going to grow, she thought. Dad's going to plant it in the yard and it'll grow so, so big.

She rushed back to her diary and wrote, "Matt and I will grow together like..." Instead of writing "avocado trees," she wrote "rosebushes." Avocadoes were okay for guacamole or sliced on top of enchiladas, but should never, she reasoned, be coupled with love. Love was forever, love was like the seasons—spring, summer, autumn, winter. She wrote: "Matt and me are going to grow together like rosebushes. We'll smell good and have pretty flowers. The bees will drink from that place." She frowned at the vagueness of "that place." She was picturing the center of the rose, but what was it called? She remembered Mr. Norman talking about plants in biology, and even speaking about roses. What was that thing called? She clacked her pen between her teeth as she struggled to remember what it was—that center place where the bees go!

Her cell phone buzzed—Matt, she hoped. But the call turned out to be from Cynthia, one of her closest friends. Monica didn't bother to answer it, certain that Cynthia was just going to ask, "What are you doing?"

Plus, she was a little mad at Cynthia. When she told

Cynthia earlier in the week that she was in love with Matt, Cynthia said only: "Let me have that cookie." They were eating lunch together, two lone birds sitting far from others—the commotion in the cafeteria was frantic as a hockey game, violent boys pushing each other. At the time, Monica felt insulted that a cookie could be more important than her sweet confession of love. In fact she snapped, "Didn't you hear me? I said I loved Matt!" At which Cynthia reached for the cookie and said, "Yeah, I heard you, girl. You don't have to get hysterical!"

Monica ignored Cynthia's call, as she had no intention of pushing her private moment with Matt to another part of her heart. She closed her diary and went outside. She looked down at her Hello Kitty wristwatch: 12:47. What should I do? she wondered, running a thumb down the spine of her diary. She figured that she could write more in her diary, and was going to do that—whenever she remembered what the center of the rose was called—when Mrs. Hendrix, an elderly neighbor, began crossing the street. She was holding a broom in her hand, and for one very mean second Monica pictured her neighbor as the Wicked Witch of the North.

Monica frowned at such an ungenerous thought. Mrs. Hendrix wasn't so much a witch as she was a bother. How many times had her dad gone over to help her change a lightbulb, hose down a wasp's nest under the eaves, fetch a newspaper from the roof, or start a troublesome mower *and* do the mowing? Also, she was such a stingy woman.

For trick-or-treat Mrs. Hendrix was known to hand out chewing gum, and not packs of gum but individual sticks. One year the miserly neighbor offered nothing more than walnuts and fistfuls of raisins.

What did she want now?

"Yoo-hoo, girl." She beckoned as she moved, turtle-like, across the street. "Can you help me?"

Monica's smile flickered as briefly as a struck match, then went out. Mrs. Hendrix was old. Still, Monica felt she had no excuse for not knowing her name. After all, they had been neighbors since Monica was four years old.

"What is it, Mrs. Hendrix?" Monica called politely. She did her best to paste a smile on her face.

Mrs. Hendrix arrived from across the street, breathing hard. She tapped her heart with an age-peppered hand. "My cat, Cecil," she wheezed. "He's in the tree."

Monica could picture her tiger-striped cat, yellowish eyes slanted and full of fury. The bully cat was renowned for thrashing other cats.

Monica asked herself: Why would I want to help that mean cat? Then she remembered her mother's advice to be nice and the world will be nice back.

"In the tree?" Monica asked.

"What?" the old woman asked, holding the broom in both hands.

"The cat's in the tree?" Monica tried again, this time in a tone of voice that suggested a holler.

"That's right," the old woman answered just as loudly.

She raised a hand and pointed. "In the backyard. I need you to help him!"

With Mrs. Hendrix shuffling behind, Monica crossed the street and headed to the backyard. When she pushed open the back gate, she found the cat not in the tree but underneath the hedge, with a bird in its mouth. Shocked by this gruesome scene, Monica cried: "Oh, my God!" The cat looked up greedily and hissed, as if to say, "You can't have any. Go get your own bird."

"You're bad!" Monica cried. "You're bad and mean!" She spanked her thighs, which prompted the cat to start slinking away with the bird. "Drop it!" she scolded. "Drop it right now!" The bird, Monica could see, was a robin and was still alive. The robin was pleading with its eyes.

"Did you say something?" Mrs. Hendrix asked as she entered the backyard, latching the gate behind her.

"Your cat was..." Monica began, then stopped herself. She couldn't possibly re-create in words the awful experience of a poor robin in the clutches of such a nasty cat. Plus, she didn't have time. She stomped her foot on the mushy lawn and yelled, "Let it go!"

The startled cat did just that—the robin, seconds earlier in death's teeth, beat its wings and soared to the roof.

"Yea," Monica sang in relief.

"Oh, Mr. Cecil," Mrs. Hendrix cried, and applauded with her fingertips. "You saved him!"

Saved him! Monica nearly blasted in anger. I saved the *bird*! She cast an angry eye at Mr. Cecil, the bully.

"Oh, Mr. Cecil," Mrs. Hendrix repeated. "You almost hurt yourself."

Monica wished to get away. She was too much in love to bother with this near fatal mauling. She gazed once again at the robin safely perched on the roof. It seemed all right, ready to fly—and it did! It tore into the sky and beyond some trees. Monica touched her heart, only seconds ago beating with fear but now slowed to its regular *thump, thump.*

"He's a rascal," Mrs. Hendrix said of her cat. "But I was thinking..."

Mrs. Hendrix had a job for Monica, one that she at her age couldn't tackle. She touched the small of her back and winced dramatically. "Oh, it's not fun being old," Mrs. Hendrix remarked, and bent over stiffly to pick up a rake. She asked Monica, giraffe tall, if she could knock down the leaves from the tree.

Be nice, Monica told herself. Just do it. Just get it over with.

For thirty minutes Monica poked the limbs with a rake, harvesting leaves that rained like confetti. She raked the burnt-brown leaves into a large pile, and refrained from frowning when Mrs. Hendrix offered her a handful of walnuts for payment. She accepted the walnuts, left the yard, and halfway down her block placed those hard nuggets all in a line on the curb. She stomped them, and tossed the meat of the walnuts onto a neighbor's lawn.

Birds need to eat, too, she told herself. They need energy in order to escape from mean cats.

But what was she to do? When she looked at her watch, she found that it was only 1:22. She had nearly an hour before she would see Matt at Starbucks, a full hour because, while their date was scheduled for two, she couldn't possibly be on time. That was against the rules, according to an advice column she had read. She had to be late by at least ten minutes but not more than twenty.

Her cell phone rang in her pocket. She brought it out: Cynthia again. She let it take a message, and decided to kill time by strolling along the canal that ran behind her house. She wished it was a river, like the ones running wildly in movies, but it was just a canal, sort of junky, with tires, car parts, barbecue grills, and whatever else, submerged in water that, when not flowing, was frothy with green yuck! Occasionally there was an old couch dumped on the weedy banks. How she loathed the debris and the spray-painted graffiti on the rocks.

I'll just pretend it's nice, she thought. I'll walk along the canal and write in my diary how beautiful the canal is. Sometimes it was okay to bend the truth, she believed.

At the canal, as expected, she found large debris—a fat refrigerator, tires, and the skeleton of a bicycle—but she also found that the autumn leaves had hidden most of the litter nicely. There were birds flitting from the trees to the bank and back. The canal, usually dry during summer, was running swiftly. The moment was pretty. She imagined tiny fish below the surface.

"Matt!" she sang, and spread her arms like bird wings. "Matt, can you hear me? I know you'll love me if you get to know me!"

Embarrassed by her outburst, Monica composed herself. What if someone behind one of those fences was spying on her? Her face, already pinkish from the cold air of November, reddened. Still, she was more convinced than ever that splashing through her heart was that red, red potion called love. She considered screaming, "I love youuuuuuu."

However, she nearly produced a scream for another reason. She recognized the robin that Mr. Cecil had nearly torn to bits.

"It's you, huh?" she called to the robin as she lifted her gaze toward the tree where the bird was perched. Most of the birds that dwelled in the trees and brush around the canal were common, dirt-colored sparrows. So she was sure that it was the same robin. The robin was saying "Thank you" in its birdy way.

The robin sprang from the tree, flew past her head, and disappeared.

"It was you," she whispered. She viewed it as a sign, a miracle perhaps. She pulled a strand of hair from her mouth. "I know it was you."

Moved to something like sadness, Monica sat down on

a fallen tree limb darkened with graffiti. She looked at her shoes, her thighs, her hands set on her thighs. I'm human, she told herself. I feel things. I hurt when I feel things. She opened her diary and wrote, "The robin I saved was just here at the canal and he was chirping, Thankyouthankyouthankyou." Examining her words, she noticed that her penmanship was full of loopy letters. She recalled a teacher describing her penmanship as romantic, because her letters were like little boats rising against an invisible onslaught of waves.

Maybe I am a romantic, she told herself. What's wrong with that? The world needs more love. She rose from the fallen tree limb, shoved the diary into the front pocket of her hoodie, and moved clumsily down the bank. She watched the water pushing along an armada of leaves, twigs, and sticks, and then grimaced with disgust at a Styrofoam ice chest floating past like an iceberg. She muttered, "People don't know where to put their garbage. They just litter!"

But her brooding lifted when she made out what looked like a frog on the other side of the canal, but might just be a clump of wet mud. She remembered reading *Frog and Toad* books when she was little, reading them a hundred times. Frog and Toad were such good friends, and lived in such a beautiful place—a book.

Monica fogged her Hello Kitty watch and cleaned its surface with her sleeve. She realized that she had only fifteen minutes to get to Starbucks. It was five to two!

She hurried from the canal, a little mad at herself because the tips of her tennis shoes were a bit muddy. She began to sprint, as she realized that she was late. What if Matt didn't wait for her? What if he arrived on time, looked around once or twice, and left to do whatever boys do when they're not with girls?

When she pulled open the door at Starbucks, she was greeted by the overpowering smell of coffee. While she was no coffee drinker, she sniffed its aroma. She next sniffed the air for the smell of a boy with his father's cologne on his neck. She looked at the six tables—no boy waiting alone—and walked behind a large display of coffee mugs. Matt wasn't there. Had he come and gone?

She got in line to order chocolate, but stepped out of line when the cashier asked, "May I help you?" She considered it rude not to wait for Matt.

She sat down at an unoccupied table. She raised her sleeve and looked at her watch: 2:12. She wasn't late at all, according to the rules of the game that girls should keep boys waiting...at least for a bit. Worried, she brought out her cell phone. She skipped over Cynthia's message and listened to a message from her mother telling her that she would be home at four, five at the latest. She shoved the phone back into her pocket and peered out the window at two boys in white T-shirts as long as dresses. The first boy wasn't Matt, and—she stood up for a better view—neither was the boy adjusting his iPod.

Back in line, she ordered a hot chocolate. She returned

to the table in small baby steps, as the chocolate was filled to the brim and was hot. To keep busy, to hear another voice other than the one inside her head, she called Cynthia, who picked up.

"Where you been?" Cynthia asked in a near holler.

"Nowhere," Monica answered vaguely. Then she said, "At the canal."

"That dirty place," Cynthia bellowed. Behind her voice was the sound of bowling pins crashing.

"It wouldn't be dirty if people didn't litter," Monica offered in return. Then she came to the point: Matt and she had a date, but he hadn't shown up. "We were supposed to meet at two," Monica began. She was prepared to fill in the details of her despair, but was put on hold. Then seconds later Cynthia said that she was going to have to call back because she had an urgent call. Cynthia hung up without a good-bye.

"And my call's not urgent?" she muttered at her cell phone. "What a friend!" When her cell phone rang seconds later—Cynthia's number came up—she pouted and shoved the cell into her pocket. She picked up her hot chocolate, sipped, and gazed at the clock behind the counter: 2:21.

At a quarter to three she left, pushing the door open with anger. Was it possible to feel any worse? When she took a step, a string of blue gum stretched from under the sole of her shoe. She scraped the gum against the edge of the curb, and cursed.

Monica returned home, but didn't go inside. She stood in front, letting her eyes dry from the tears that had rolled down her cheeks. She feared her mother's worry and the one question that might really bring her again to gushing tears: "What's wrong, honey?" Monica made out her father passing by the front window, and imagined that someone walking by might think that they had a teenage daughter who was happy.

But she wasn't happy! If she were a cloud, she would rumble with thunder and lightning. She would throw down on her neighborhood a cold rain, hail maybe, yes, hail the size of softballs. She pictured Matt popping a baseball glove and saying, "I got it, I got it!" Yeah, right! Let him try to catch the hail I would throw down on him.

Monica felt pathetic. She blew into her cupped hands, her frosty breath rising like fog between her laced fingers. Although it was getting cold, she didn't feel like climbing the steps, wiping the soles of her shoes, and calling in a false happiness, "I'm home."

She walked down the street. With the sun at her back, her shadow lengthened. The wind cut through the trees, loosening the last of the fall leaves. In front of one house she shuddered at the sight of twin rosebushes that would greet visitors as they walked up the pebbly walk. She stopped and scowled at the rosebushes. Denuded of leaves, the rosebushes were really like sticks. Without their scented flowers they weren't even pretty. They were full of thorns that could make you bleed.

At the end of the block she paused as two boys approached on bicycles. They were pumping hard and yelling at each other—something about a football.

"Matt," she muttered, and snorted. "It's Matt and his stupid friend Robert."

Matt rode past without a hello, but he circled back when he recognized Monica. He stopped in front of her, breathing hard.

"I thought you were going to meet me at two," she declared right away. She warned herself not to break down and sob.

Matt straddled his bike. His face was red from the cold and his hair was full of grass. His nostrils were wet.

"I'm sorry," Matt said, and ran a finger across his nostrils. He looked at his finger and wiped the clear residue on his pants. "There was something I had to do."

Monica almost snapped, You mean be with Robert? You rather would be with Robert than me? Instead she stated flatly, "You stood me up. You said you were going to be at Starbucks."

Cloud-like remorse passed over Matt's small eyes, but immediately cleared up. "It was my bad," he apologized. "I want to, you know, like get together." He turned his head and gave Robert a sneer—or was it a smile? Monica wasn't sure. He returned his attention to Monica. "I'm like really sorry. I wanted to go, but I couldn't. I got something to do." He made a phone of his hands near his ear and added, "I'll call."

He tore off, his T-shirt flapping from the force of his pedaling, before Monica could scold, "Don't bother."

That night in bed she wrote in her diary, "Today was really, really bad. I was supposed to meet Matt, but he was so busy playing stupid football. I'm going to forget him. I'll see him at school but will pretend he's invisible—no, pretend that he's a worm." She covered the page with daggers through a row of hearts.

Sunday morning. Fog pressed against all their windows. She was alone in her pajamas, as her parents had gone to eight o'clock Mass. On the sofa, with her stuffed unicorn on her lap, Monica sipped hot chocolate and made her last entry in her diary. She wrote about how boys were immature, if not sometimes stupid, and without manners. Why did they always have to wipe their boogers on their pants? She wrote in her most loopy penmanship the word "good-bye" and closed her diary for the last time.

She dressed and went outside by way of the kitchen. She opened the back gate and stood on the bike path that ran along the canal. The fog was thick as it swirled in front of her.

"It's so cold," she complained with a shiver. She breathed into her hands, which were already pink, and galloped down the bike path to build up warmth. She slowed to a walk when she caught sight of a small metal bridge, the place where she used to throw flowers into the water. When she was really little she thought that the flowers would be carried away and plant themselves on the edge of the canal. There the flowers would multiply and spread prettiness until the world was bright with flowers.

But at thirteen Monica could only lament that her childhood had flowed away like a river. She walked past the usual debris—the piled tires, a broken chest of drawers, and a recliner with its guts spilled out. A stray cat looked at her from atop a pile of discarded lumber. Spooked for no reason, it ran away.

On the bridge Monica gazed down at the water, which was moving leaves and twigs, yellowish foam, and litter. She couldn't help but think of the canal as a big, dirty vein carrying away all the dirty things of the world. Where did it end? In a fishless lake? The sea?

In thoughtless anger, she flung her diary into the canal. But instead of hitting water and starting the slow process of sinking, the thing she had cared about more than anything landed on a pile of concrete in the middle of the canal.

"Oh," she muttered. Her fingers went to her mouth as the pages of her diary flapped like birds' wings. "Darn it," she growled, mortified that her precious diary was sitting on a pile of concrete. To a passerby, it might look like another piece of litter. But it wasn't litter. It was a hundred—no, more!—pages of her feelings!

She ran off the bridge to the bank, picked up a stick, and tried to knock the diary off the pile into the water. I can't reach it, she bawled in her heart. She next aimed a couple of rocks at it, but she couldn't hit her target.

Frustrated, she cursed. She kicked a potato chip bag in anger and tossed a soda bottle into the canal, prompting a frog hiding in the weeds to jump and flop into the water.

She feared that the diary would just remain there on the pile of concrete, visible to the whole world! That is, until a hard rain raised the level of the canal and it floated off, like a little boat, and eventually sank to the bottom. Only then would her words and feelings blur forever.

"Oh," she repeated with a sob. "I shouldn't have done it."

"Done what?" a voice asked.

Monica turned. A boy, partially lost in fog, was standing before her. When he took two steps toward her his entire shape appeared: He was taller than she. His face was smooth, but his jutting jaw was like one of those pieces of concrete—hard.

"My book..." Monica began, pointing with the stick.

The boy came down from the bike path to the bank and stood so close that she, a giraffe of a girl, had to look up at him. She swallowed. He was handsome, strong, and older, with light hair on his chin.

"I dropped it," Monica lied. She could hardly look at him, this handsome boy.

Without a word the boy took off his shoes and socks, rolled up his pants legs, and waded into the water, showing only the slightest reaction to the cold. He retrieved the diary, looked briefly at the cover with its array of flowers, but didn't open it. Monica could tell he knew that it was a diary, not a book, and knew there was a story within its pages. If he asked, Monica would tell him.

When he handed it back to her, their hands touched. Monica's face began to warm, and a smile not unlike the sun appeared. She lowered her gaze and was suddenly no longer the tall giraffe of her father's dream but a bashful lamb.

"Thank you," Monica said, pulling her hair behind her ear. She couldn't resist smiling at him, thus giving away her feelings. She asked his name.

"Michael," he answered.

Monica felt weak. She had always wanted to know a boy named Michael. When she asked clumsily, "What are you doing out here?" she almost crumbled from his answer.

"I'm planting seeds," he answered. He peeled his backpack from his shoulders and brought out a clear plastic bag of seeds. "They're native flowers, mostly poppies. They'll flower in spring if I plant them now."

Oh, my God, she thought. A boy planting flowers? She bit her lower lip to keep from smiling foolishly. Her voice lifted brightly as she said that some people were fond of roses, but poppies were her favorite flower.

"Can I help?" Monica asked after she had climbed the few steps from the bank to the bike path.

"Sure," Michael replied.

She told him that she was in eighth grade and that the thing in her hands was not a book but her diary. She told him that she had thrown it into the canal because she was mad at someone.

The older boy didn't ask who.

Michael, she learned as they began to walk side by side, was fifteen, two years older than she, and had biked from across town. He was a member of the high school environmental club and was getting extra credit for his work.

"But I'm doing it because I like it," Michael admitted. "I want to study botany in college." He pointed beyond the bridge shrouded in fog and said, "Let's start over there."

"Okay," Monica whispered. "Yeah, we should start over there."

They descended to the canal bank. Michael gave Monica a small ziplock bag filled with seeds. She shook it and listened to its maracas-like music. She was happy. She could disappear in this thick fog and never come out, as long as she was with this boy.

The two walked along the canal bank, bending every four or five feet to push seeds into the wet mud. By May the first poppy would burst open, and bees would swarm the center—the pistil, she suddenly remembered—for its sweet nectar.

Dirty Talk

Bored almost to the point of tears, Tiffany Tafolla sat on the living room couch with a pillow on her lap. She looked at the mantel clock: 10:37. She sighed and gazed out the front window. She wished *something* would happen. A cold Saturday morning in January, the fog as gray as cement. How did people drive through such thick fog?

She recalled seeing an old science fiction movie with her Uncle Richard. It was about fog that killed people, and it was one of Uncle Richard's favorites from the 1950s. As she finished her box of Milk Duds she knew that the movie was no good, no matter how much Uncle called it a classic. At age nine she swore none too quietly, "This movie is *@!*." Her uncle, who had also been devouring Milk Duds in the dark, halted his pleasurable munching and glared down at his niece. He licked his lips, as if preparing to scold her for her language. But he only winced, shook his head at his niece, and wiped her mouth clean of chocolate.

That was four years ago. Now, on the couch, Tiffany muttered, "That girl looks like a duck. Her *#&@!* legs are too short!" She was watching a rerun of *Dance Your Ass Off,* and Tiffany thought nothing of her outburst. The girl she cussed at deserved it! She had no business on television, especially with such a great partner! The guy was hot!

"I'm bored," Tiffany admitted after releasing a yawn that could have inflated a balloon. She tossed the pillow in her lap aside, spooking awake her cat, Maxi, and got up from the couch. She reached for the remote control on the coffee table before pressing "off"—the girl with short legs disappeared.

She was four steps into the kitchen and ready to confront the breakfast dishes, her one chore for the day, when her cell phone rang.

"**&#," Tiffany muttered. She pulled the cell phone from her pants pocket and checked the phone number: Beatrice Fuentes, her best friend. She took the call. "Hey, girl, what the +!@!*. You were supposed to call at nine." They had plans to go the mall and scour the stores for good-looking guys. It would be something fun to do on a winter day.

"You know what that &!@!* Manuel did?" Beatrice bawled. "He's sharing that *!@!* photo he took of me eating a burrito. It's on his Facebook page!"

"Shysty rat!" Tiffany slurred in anger, her face heating up beneath a layer of multicolored cosmetics. She scowled as she remembered the photo. Beatrice was struggling with a burrito—the cheese was clinging to her chin like dental floss—when Manuel, her goofy boyfriend, clicked the photo with his cell phone. And now he had posted it on the *!@!* Internet!

"I hate him!" Beatrice bellowed. "I'm never going to talk to him again. He's a *!@*! fool!"

"Yeah, he is," Tiffany agreed as she looked down at Maxi purring at her ankles. She tickled the cat's scruff with her toes. "I got to clean up the kitchen, but I'll be over in an hour." She snapped shut her phone in anger, muttered *$%@*!" and, rolling up the sleeves of her red hoodie, faced the dishes piled high as an Egyptian pyramid. She squirted blue detergent into a plastic tub. She picked up a sponge—one side was spongy and the other side rough. Her makeup began to loosen from the steam of the hot water and her anger at Manuel for pulling such a trashy trick. How dare he put that image on Facebook! "That's his girlfriend," she roared to the black frying pan. "What's wrong with him?" she asked the plates with hardened egg. "How could he do that?" she yelled at the spoons and forks. Her heart beat angrily as she pushed the *frijoles* down the garbage disposal. She ground them for a long minute.

Finished, Tiffany reapplied her makeup, sprayed her neck with perfume, and put on a long wool coat that reached below her knees. She pulled on a Raiders cap and black gloves, and made her exit.

"Man, it's cold," Tiffany complained with a shiver from the porch. Nevertheless, it was good to get out of the house and have a purpose greater than watching television. She would run over to Beatrice's house and make her feel better. Tiffany spanked her two gloved hands together and sprinted off the porch, leaping with her arms out like wings. She felt happy doing this, the spring and leap off the porch. If only she could really fly!

"*!@!*," she heard from the neighbor, Mr. Ramirez, a heavyset man who could break a sweat just picking up a tool from the ground. He was in his driveway fooling with his pickup truck. In the bed of his truck sat Frisko, his pit bull rescued from the animal shelter. Frisko sported a pirate's patch over his permanently injured eye and a collar studded with nails.

"Hey, Mr. Ramirez," Tiffany greeted him, her white breath unrolling like a cloud from her mouth. "It's =*&! cold, huh?"

"You got that right," he hollered from behind the small wooden fence that ran between the properties. He complained about the starter and, gazing into his toolbox, muttered, "Where's my socket wrench? *!@*!"

"Do you think Frisko's cold?" Tiffany asked. She felt sorry for the dog because, unlike Maxi, he had to sleep outside on an old army blanket.

Mr. Ramirez looked momentarily at the dog. "*!@!* no. The dude is built for cold."

Tiffany walked across the frozen lawn, turned and walked backward a few steps, her house slowly disappearing in the fog. Down the street she ran into Mrs. Clarke, her former baby-sitter, who had spent a few months in jail for passing bad checks. But that temporary lapse of good judgment didn't color Tiffany's opinion of Mrs. Clarke. No, everyone was doing bad—passing worthless checks, making late rent payments, and committing outright thievery. Only last week one of their neighbors caught a teenager breaking into his house. The multitasking teenager, the neighbor reported to the police, was on his cell phone talking to a friend while he was shimmying through the back bedroom window.

"A $&*!=* cold day, huh?" Mrs. Clarke offered up as conversation. Bundled in a couple of coats, she was raking leaves in her front yard. When she smiled she revealed an empty space where a tooth should be. Her ratty hair looked as if it had been pulled at by a blackbird.

"Yeah, it is," Tiffany answered in return. "I can hardly see where I'm *!@*! walking." She laughed. She sprinted down the street, trying to build up heat beneath her coat. But she stopped when an elderly woman asked in Spanish if Tiffany could help her.

"Like what?" Tiffany asked roughly.

"*El árbol de naranja*," she began to explain. She

pointed to the tree on the side of her house. "Would you be a dear and pick a few for me?"

Tiffany eyed the house and the string of Christmas lights hanging from the eaves. There was an orderly squad of cactus plants in coffee and soup cans on the porch. And were those two bulky plastic garbage bags filled with aluminum cans? Bundled cardboard for recycling? Her parents had warned her about such a ploy—a nice woman begging for help and the next moment you, an innocent victim, are tied up in a van and going somewhere nasty.

"Nah, I ain't got time," Tiffany answered. Under her breath she swore, "*!@! no."

Tiffany walked away, throwing back a few Tic Tac breath mints. But as she sucked on those wintry pellets, she became troubled by her manners. The old lady could have been her grandmother—she was Mexican and brown as a penny. She had long, ropy braids like her grandmother, too. Why did I do that? she wondered. She was just a little *viejita*. She just wanted a couple of oranges from her tree. Tiffany spat the Tic Tacs from her mouth. She didn't know why she did that, either.

"Whatever," Tiffany concluded, feeling a brief pang of remorse as she walked down the street.

A few minutes later she was at Beatrice's house. She rapped on the front door where a plastic Christmas wreath still hung, and pushed the door open when no one answered. Her face immediately enveloped by heat from the over-warm living room. Tiffany expected Beatrice's eyes to be pooled with tears when she arrived. Where was the mascara running like sludge down her cheeks? The pouting mouth? Where were the shoulder heaving sobs and the box of Kleenex on the coffee table? Instead, Beatrice's eyes were bright with laughter.

"You should see what that #@!*# girl is wearing," Beatrice said, her hand on her stomach.

Tiffany glanced at the program on television. A chubby girl in an orange tank top was standing in the three-sixty-degree mirror. Tiffany had a tank top not unlike the girl's somewhere in her drawers. But on her it looked cute. On this old imitation Barbie with stringy hair—ugly.

"I thought you would be all sad?" Tiffany asked as she sat down next to Beatrice on the couch, ready to raise her arms and hug her best friend. She rested her hand on Beatrice's knee.

"Nah," Beatrice answered without looking at her. Her eyes were on the television and her smile was undulating like a wave.

This was not what Tiffany expected. No, she expected a heart-to-heart talk—and she would have it! Tiffany took the remote from the coffee table and pressed the off button. The chubby girl, flanked by Stacy and Clinton from *What Not to Wear*, disappeared, though their images clung to the back of Tiffany's mind. Right then she decided to get rid of her orange tank top.

Beatrice turned to Tiffany, her mouth open and snarling. "Why did you *!@*! do that? I was watching!"

"I want to hear about Manuel," Tiffany answered, scooting a few inches from Beatrice, who scooted a few more inches away. It looked like a face-off.

"Hear *!$%@*! what?" Beatrice tried to swipe the remote from Tiffany's hand, but Tiffany was quick enough to swing it behind her back.

"Give it to me!" Beatrice scolded. "I mean it!"

"Nah, tell me first."

"Give it to me, I said!"

Tiffany didn't like the rage on her best friend's face, or her struggle with Beatrice's arms snaking around her waist trying to get the remote. Beatrice seemed genuinely mad, but about what? That she had turned off the television? Still, Tiffany risked repeating the question. "I want to hear about Manuel." She was going to add how Manuel was such a *!&*!, but she decided that she should just keep those words inside her.

Beatrice stopped, caught her breath, and softened. Her hands came to her mouth as she hid her smile. She bowed her head and stomped her feet on the carpet. She looked up at Tiffany. "I'm going to be famous."

Tiffany offered a confused look.

"Like really famous," Beatrice said as she bounced on the couch. She explained that within twenty-four hours Manuel's photo of her eating that cheesy burrito jumped from Manuel's cell phone to a friend's cell phone. The image jumped like a virus from cell phone to cell phone— all this before Manuel posted it on Facebook, where it was being eyeballed around the clock. Beatrice had received phone calls and text messages confirming sightings in Rhode Island. There was a chance that her image would leap over to England by nightfall.

"That's terrible," Tiffany remarked.

"Terrible?" Beatrice arched her eyebrows. "It's like everyone's going to know my face."

"But with a string of @#!&! cheese hanging from your chin?"

"Yeah, but still!"

"Still what? Don't you think it's like ##@!& embarrassing?" Tiffany peeled off her gloves, as if getting ready for a bare-knuckled fight with Beatrice about how embarrassing it was.

"Tiffany, my face is going everywhere. People will be seeing me internationally." She reached down to a bowl of peanuts and threw a few into her mouth. She spoke with her mouth open, revealing the crunched, semi-crunched, and un-crunched peanuts. "It's like I'm finally going to be famous, like that girl on television."

Tiffany remembered the chubby girl in the orange tank top. If that was fame, Tiffany figured, they could have it.

Silence filled the room.

"What's your *!@*&! problem?" Beatrice finally asked. "And give me the remote!"

Tiffany was hurt. She had walked in the terrible cold to comfort her best friend, and now that friend was scolding her? "I was just trying to be supportive."

Beatrice snapped on the television. Stacy and Clinton were dumping clothes into a garbage can, and criticizing the woman in the orange tank top. Beatrice hoisted a smile to her face.

"I got to go," Tiffany said in a hurt voice. Her friend didn't seem to need comforting. *What Not to Wear* could do that for her.

"Nah, girl—don't go!" Beatrice apologized for her outburst.

Tiffany felt a little better and sat back down. She scratched a mustard stain on the leather couch. She flicked the flakes into an ashtray on the coffee table. "Are we going to go?" Tiffany asked.

"Go where?" Beatrice asked, genuinely puzzled by the question.

"To the mall."

"Can't," Beatrice replied. She reached for another handful of peanuts. She poured a few into her mouth, chewed a little, shook the remaining ones in her palm like dice, and said, "I got to take care of Jenny's baby."

Jenny was Beatrice's older sister. She had the baby with a guy who was now in prison—two years to pump weights for stealing a Hummer, a vehicle so poor on gas mileage they laughed that car dealers couldn't give it away.

"Jenny's staying with us," Beatrice remarked.

"Your sister?" Tiffany looked around. "Where is she? Asleep?" Jenny was known to party until dawn.

"At the mall or something," Beatrice answered. She tossed the remaining peanuts into her mouth. "The baby's asleep."

Just then, Jenny's baby came tottering into the living room. Her eyes were large and her light brown hair tousled. Her cheeks were pink from just waking up.

"She is so, so cute!" Tiffany sang. "Come here, sweetie." Tiffany raised her arms for the baby to come.

But the baby just stood here. She yawned and rubbed her eyes with her fists.

"You can't get any cuter! I swear!" The baby's about two, Tiffany figured. "What's her name?"

"Maria," Beatrice answered, and frowned. "Give me a *!@*! break! Ain't there enough Marias in the *$@*! world?"

Tiffany stiffened at her best friend's outburst. It was cruel and ugly. "No, we need all the precious Marias in the world. It's a classic name."

"Classic?" Beatrice muttered.

"Classic and symbolic," Tiffany defended herself.

"Whatever." Beatrice sulked, slouched into the couch, and changed the channel.

Tiffany was irate. How could she think of her niece as just another Maria? She swallowed the cuss words that almost shot out like lightning in Beatrice's direction. How dare she speak about her little niece in such a manner! Instead she resolved to be calm, and asked, "Does she talk yet?"

"Like a *$!@# parrot," Beatrice answered as she sat up. She made cooing sounds at the baby. "Maria want a cracker? Maria want a peanut?"

Maria clapped her hands and did a little jig, turning in a circle like a toy. Her large eyes squinted. Her smile revealed her tiny, white teeth. She then ran to Beatrice, who hugged her and pushed a peanut into Maria's mouth. The smiling baby began to chew on the peanut and immediately began to choke.

"Baby's okay?" Tiffany asked, her brow pleated in worry.

The baby's oval face began to turn red and her eyes, already large, seemed to get even larger. Drool seeped from her lower lip.

"Are you okay, Maria?" Tiffany asked as she went to her knees and placed a hand behind the baby's back. She tapped the baby's back and said, "Cough it up. Be a good girl and cough it up." Tiffany wiped the drool on her sleeve.

The baby appeared startled. A pinkish hand went to her mouth and came out slimy.

"She can't breathe!" Tiffany shouted. She rubbed the baby's back and tapped it softly and then harder when the baby's face began to turn purple and a single tear began to slip down her cheek.

"Do something!" Beatrice cried as she leaped from the couch onto the floor. "Jenny's going to be mad!"

Tiffany turned the baby upside down like a saltshaker.

She cried in panic, "Come on, Maria, cough it up," and drummed her fist against her back until the peanut flopped onto the carpet. Tiffany righted the baby and set her on the couch. The purple in her face slowly drained to a pinkish flush while she gasped for air.

"Man, you scared us," Beatrice yelled at Maria. She dabbed roughly at the drool on the baby's chin. "Don't do that again!"

The baby rubbed tears from her eyes. She sneezed and put her fingers into her mouth.

"Poor thing," Tiffany said in relief. "She could have choked and died." She could feel her heart racing, and noticed that her hands were shaking. She locked her hands together, but they still trembled.

The baby pushed out her pudgy arm and opened her palm. She made a noise with her lips that to Tiffany sounded like "Please."

"No, no peanuts for the bad girl," Beatrice scolded. But she reached for the bowl of peanuts and pushed a handful into her own mouth.

"She's not bad. It was just an accident." Tiffany pouted at the baby, cooed precious words, and took her hand into hers as she sat down next to her. She lifted the baby into her lap. "Huh, sweetie, just a little accident. A boo-boo."

The baby looked up at Tiffany and, reaching upward with her sticky hands, cooed sweetly, "*!@#*"

Beatrice laughed and pointed. "Did you hear her? This little gangsta girl's already using bad words!"

Shocked, Tiffany gazed at little Maria's mouth. How could such a sweet, darling thing cuss? She lifted the baby from her lap and onto the couch.

Maria smiled and repeated, "*!#@*!" She clapped and smiled. She shimmied off the couch and helped herself to the soda on the coffee table.

"Are you going to let her drink soda?" Tiffany herself liked sodas, but knew enough about healthy habits to understand that a soda was really a poor choice for a growing baby. "Don't you think she should drink milk or juice?"

"She can drink anything she wants," Beatrice replied defensively. "Huh, home girl? Show Tiffany how you dance."

Baby Maria began to wag her head side to side in imitation of Beatrice towering above her. Maria then began to move slowly around the coffee table, clicking her fingers. Beatrice clapped her hands overhead, the baby following along. When Beatrice shook her bottom, the baby did the same. Then the baby tripped and knocked the glass of soda off the coffee table.

"*!@$&!" Beatrice yelled. "Look at what you done!" She raised the flat of her hand and yelled, "I should spank you."

The baby ran from the living room.

"You wouldn't spank her," Tiffany said.

"But look at what she did!" The soda was quickly disappearing into the carpet. Beatrice hurried to the kitchen for a dish towel.

Tiffany began to slip on her gloves. I'm out of here, she thought. She felt remorseful and sick, but for what? What was it exactly? That Beatrice was proud of her burrito-eating image spreading across the country, or the soda-drinking baby who already had bad words in her vocabulary?

"Where you going?" Beatrice asked as she returned to the living room holding a damp and twisted dish towel.

"Home to do some work," Tiffany answered, with a little push behind her words.

"You're jealous, huh?" Beatrice snarled. She began to twist the towel.

"About what?" Tiffany asked, one hand on the door-knob. She was hurt by her friend's tone of voice. She also thought for a second that Beatrice might snap the dish towel at her.

"About me." There was an anger pushing out of Beatrice's eyeballs. Would smoke from her nostrils follow? "It's because I got Manuel and you ain't got nobody. It's because everyone's going to know me."

"Eating a burrito? With cheese hanging from your chin?" Tiffany asked, anger building up like a fire in her own heart. "Is that what you want to be known for? Get a life!"

"Jealous," Beatrice hurled at her friend. She snapped open the dish towel and knelt to clean up the spilled soda. "That's what you are—jealous!" In a frenzy, she began to rub the spill.

Tiffany turned and opened the door, the cold, wintry air rushing against her face. She left as Beatrice continued to heave insults about how stuck-up Tiffany was.

"You can think what you want," Tiffany tossed at Beatrice, and closed the door behind her. She hurried down the street in scissoring steps that could have cut metal.

The fog was thick, even thicker than earlier. A pair of yellowish headlights appeared in the road, briefly lighting up what was for Tiffany a dark day. She had lost her friend, and feared for baby Maria. She imagined the toddler eating peanuts and drinking a soda, while seated inches from the blaring television. If only I could rescue her, Tiffany thought. If only I could stop her from saying those bad words.

Tiffany thought about how she herself learned them. How did she start? In the theater with her Uncle Richard? From her parents, who sometimes used profanity? She hated herself, and hated herself even more as she walked toward the house where the old woman with the orange tree had asked her for help.

"She's a nice woman," Tiffany told herself. "She just wanted oranges." Right there, Tiffany promised herself not to talk to Beatrice, even if she became famous. Her lower lip was trembling as she began to cry. She closed her eyes and saw little Maria clapping her hands over her head. The poor thing, she thought.

A car passed, again lighting up the foggy day. But the light receded, and she was once again alone in the fog.

I'll just use nice words, she told herself. Words like *rose, garden, pretty clouds, jasmine,* and *love.* She could feel her face lift in happiness as she recited these words. She thought of the *other* words—the cuss words, the profanity, the hip-hop slang, the funky language of the school yard—and she could feel her mood darken. She could even feel her face change into something hateful.

Tiffany stopped in front of the old woman's house. There was a yellowish glow behind the front window and the faint lilt of Mexican music. Without being asked a second time, she took it upon herself to pick those oranges. She entered the yard, got a bench leaning against a fence, and boosted herself into the orange tree.

"Kitten," she piped as she picked the first orange. "Candy," she hummed when she plucked the second one. "Jam, birthday, pony," she said as she plucked one orange after another, until the pockets of her big coat were filled and her mouth was singing a new vocabulary.